Antiques Ho-Ho-Homicide

A Trash 'n' Treasures Mystery

Barbara Allan

KENSINGTON BOOKS
http://www.kensingtonbooks.com

KENSINGTON BOOKS are published by

Kensington Publishing Corp.
119 West 40th Street
New York, NY 10018

All Kensington titles, imprints, and distributed lines are available at special quantity discounts for bulk purchases for sales promotion, premiums, fund-raising, educational, or institutional use. Special book excerpts or customized printings can also be created to fit specific needs. For details, write or phone the office of the Kensington Special Sales Manager: Attn. Special Sales Department. Kensington Publishing Corp., 119 West 40th Street, New York, NY 10018. Phone: 1-800-221-2647.

ISBN-13: 978-1-4967-1165-6
ISBN-10: 1-4967-1165-3
First Kensington Mass Market Edition: October 2018

10 9 8 7 6 5 4 3 2 1

Printed in the United States of America

HIGHEST PRAISE FOR THE TRASH 'N' TREASURES MYSTERY SERIES

ANTIQUES FRAME

"A conversational writing style, with both Vivian and Brandy sharing the narration, adds to the appeal here, along with the well-drawn mother-daughter relationship and the many details of the antique business."—***Booklist***

"Appealing . . . live-wire Vivian sets out to clear her daughter's name with her usual gusto and risible results."—***Publishers Weekly***

"A laugh a page with larger-than-most characters who are still believable. If you like mysteries on the funny side of life, this series is a great read."—***RT Book Reviews*, 4 Stars**

"The amusingly ditzy duo manages to solve yet another case."—***Kirkus Reviews***

"A fast-moving and frequently hilarious mystery concoction."—***Bill Crider's Pop Culture Magazine***

ANTIQUES FATE

"Well-drawn characters . . . fun to read."
—***Booklist***

ANTIQUES SWAP

"Brandy and Vivian are engaging, well-drawn characters, and their first-person narration is

fun to read. Quirky secondary characters add to the appeal of this humorous cozy mystery."
—***Booklist***

ANTIQUES CON

"Endlessly amusing . . . A fashion-obsessed team of sleuthing antiques dealers takes on the Big Apple."—***Kirkus Reviews***

"Tips about comics collecting add to the cozy fun."—***Publishers Weekly***

"Allan's madcap series provides non-stop humor as well as a logical, tangled mystery. This is a fun, fast mystery that shows Allan at the top of her game."—***RT Book Reviews*, 4½ stars**

"A hilarious collaborative effort by Barbara and Max Allan Collins. Antiquing tips included."
—***Library Journal***

"If you're tired of the dour, dark and brooding mysteries so prevalent today, give your soul a little lift with this cheeky and fun series."
—***Bookgasm***

"This fun, fast mystery shows Allan at the top of her game."—***RT Book Reviews, 4½ stars***

ANTIQUES CHOP

"The characters shine with brassy humor."
—***Publishers Weekly***

"Plenty of suspects, a red herring or two, and lots of laughs along the way. . . Read the book. You'll have a great time, and you can thank me later."—*Bill Crider's Pop Culture Magazine*

ANTIQUES DISPOSAL

"The book is so damn funny, I honestly couldn't put it down. Hey, did I mention there are recipes for chocolate brownies in it? Now how can you go wrong with that?"
—*Pulp Fiction Reviews*

"A ditzy mother-daughter duo, a denouement out of Nero Wolfe, antiquing tips . . . an amusing mystery."—*Kirkus Reviews*

"Breezy, written with admirable wit . . . .a wacky, lightweight romp perfect for an evening's escapism. This series is just pure fun, and the humor is a treat."—*Somebody Dies*

"Treasure, yes. Trash, no. A madcap adventure; a bright, funny, and fast-moving mystery; all good fun and well-played . . . another charmer for Mr. and Mrs. Collins."
—*Jerry's House of Everything*

"Here's something to brighten your day . . . very funny, with lots of great dialogue. There's even a Nero Wolfe homage, along with a cliffhanger ending . . . good news for us fans."—*Bill Crider's Pop Culture Magazine*

"This humorous cozy is framed by life in small-town Iowa and teems with quirky characters."
—Booklist

"A charming story and a fun summer read."
—A Book for Today

"This is such a fun book to read. It was hilarious and had me laughing out loud many times. Highly recommended for cozy mystery fans and fans of those storage unit auction shows on TV."***—Daisy's Book Journal***

ANTIQUES KNOCK-OFF

"An often amusing tale complete with lots of antiques-buying tips and an ending that may surprise you."***—Kirkus Reviews***

"Quirky . . . Throw in a touch of Mafia menace, a New Age hypnotist with a herd of cats, a very tasty recipe, and some smart tips on antique collecting, and you've got yourself a sure-fire winner."***—Publishers Weekly***

"If you like laugh-out-loud funny mysteries, this will make your day. Place your bets on this screwball comedy cozy where the clues are thick and the mother-daughter dynamics are off the charts."***—Romantic Times Book Reviews,* 4.5 stars**

"Stop shoveling snow, take time to chuckle: *Antiques Knock-Off* is a fitting antidote to any seasonal blues, putting life into perspective as more than a little crazy, and worth laughing about."—***Kingdom Books***

"Great reading, very funny. In fact, the first page of this book is so funny and so well done that I just had to stop reading for a while and admire it. Highly recommended."
—***Bill Crider's Pop Culture Magazine***

"Scenes of Midwestern small-town life, informative tidbits about the antiques business, and clever dialog make this essential for those who like unusual amateur sleuths."
—***Library Journal***

ANTIQUES BIZARRE

"Auction tips and a recipe for spicy beef stew enhance this satirical cozy."—***Publishers Weekly***

"If you delight in the absurd and enjoy manic humor, you'll treasure the Trash 'n' Treasure mysteries."—***Mystery Scene***

"Genuinely funny . . . another winner! The *Trash 'n' Treasures* books have to be the funniest mystery series going."—***Somebody Dies***

"I love the books by 'Barbara Allan.' Great characters drive this series, and the research about the antiques really adds to the story. It's fun reading and the mystery is terrific."
—***Crimespree***

ANTIQUES FLEE MARKET

"Lively…this bubbly tongue-in-cheek cozy also includes flea market shopping tips and a recipe."—***Publishers Weekly***

"A fast-paced plot, plenty of tongue-in-cheek humor, and tips on antiques collecting will keep readers engaged."—***Library Journal***

"Top pick! This snappy mystery has thrills, laugh-out-loud moments and amazingly real relationships."—***Romantic Times Book Reviews*, 4.5 stars**

"This is surely one of the funniest cozy series going."—***Ellery Queen Mystery Magazine***

"Marvelous dialogue, great characters, and a fine murder mystery."
—reviewingtheevidince.com

"Very engaging, very funny, with amusing dialogue and a couple of nice surprises. Next time you need a laugh, check it out."—***Bill Crider's Pop Culture Magazine***

ANTIQUES MAUL

"Charming. . . a laugh-out-loud-funny mystery."—***Romantic Times* (four stars)**

ANTIQUES ROADKILL

"Brandy, her maddening mother, her uptight sister, and all the denizens of their small Iowa town are engaging and utterly believable as they crash through a drugs and antiques scam on the Mississippi. Anyone like me, who's blown the car payment on a killer outfit, will love the bonus of Brandy's clothes obsession."—**Sara Paretsky**

"If you're either a mystery reader or an antiques hunter, and especially if you're both, *Antiques Roadkill* is your book! This is the start of what's sure to be a terrific new series. Grab it up!"—**S. J. Rozan**

"Cozy mystery fans will love this down-to-earth heroine with the wry sense of humor and a big heart."—**Nancy Pickard**

"With its small town setting and cast of quirky characters, *Antiques Roadkill* is fun from start to finish. Dive in and enjoy."—**Laurien Berenson**

"Brandy and her eccentric mother Vivian make an hilarious and improbable team of snoops as they encounter the seamier side of the antiques trade in this delightful debut. *Antiques Roadkill* will certainly make you think twice about those family treasures in your attic."—**Joan Hess**

"Terrific. It's funny, witty, irreverent. From the opening page to the very last, the distinctive voice in *Antiques Roadkill* pulls you in and never lets go."—**T. J. MacGregor**

"Enormously entertaining."—***Ellery Queen Mystery Magazine***

"Cute, but with an edge."—***Quad-City Times***

"Niftily plotted . . . believable characters who are just offbeat enough . . . The story moves at a brisk pace, aided by Brandy's engaging voice, a realistic view of small towns, and an astute look at family friction."—***South Florida Sun-Sentinel***

"A clever new series [that] taps into the interests of cozy-readers . . . *Antiques Roadkill* is a true find."—***Mystery Scene***

"Amateur sleuths will enjoy this light-hearted whodunit."—***The Tapestry***

Also by Barbara Allan

ANTIQUES ROADKILL
ANTIQUES MAUL
ANTIQUES FLEE MARKET
ANTIQUES BIZARRE
ANTIQUES KNOCK-OFF
ANTIQUES DISPOSAL
ANTIQUES CHOP
ANTIQUES CON
ANTIQUES SWAP
ANTIQUES FRAME
ANTIQUES WANTED
ANTIQUES FATE

By Barbara Collins

TOO MANY TOMCATS
(short story collection)

By Barbara and Max Allan Collins

REGENERATION
BOMBSHELL
MURDER—HIS AND HERS
(short story collection)

Contents

Antiques Slay Ride

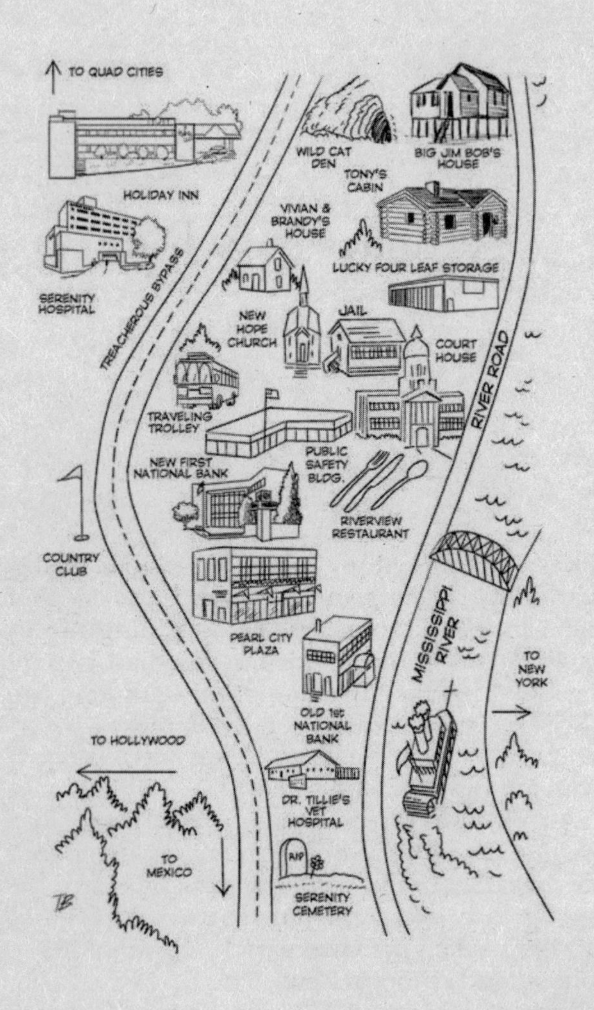
TO QUAD CITIES
WILD CAT DEN
BIG JIM BOB'S HOUSE
TONY'S CABIN
HOLIDAY INN
VIVIAN & BRANDY'S HOUSE
LUCKY FOUR LEAF STORAGE
SERENITY HOSPITAL
TREACHEROUS BYPASS
NEW HOPE CHURCH
JAIL
COURT HOUSE
RIVER ROAD
TRAVELING TROLLEY
PUBLIC SAFETY BLDG.
NEW FIRST NATIONAL BANK
RIVERVIEW RESTAURANT
COUNTRY CLUB
MISSISSIPPI RIVER
PEARL CITY PLAZA
TO NEW YORK
OLD 1st NATIONAL BANK
TO HOLLYWOOD
DR. TILLIE'S VET HOSPITAL
RIP
TO MEXICO
SERENITY CEMETERY

Chapter One

Nestled All Snug

I was dreaming in my warm bed, visions of sugarplums dancing in my head, when Mother came into my room, rudely awakening me by banging on an old toy drum. She had bought the thing for the six-year-old me on a long-ago Christmas as a measure of self-defense—an attempt to keep her pots and pans (and spoons) from getting further dented.

An old trick on her part—I had long since learned to work the noise of that toy drum into my dreams, but just as the sugarplums were lining up in a row right out of *Babes in Toyland*, Mother yanked the covers back, exposing me to cold air and colder reality.

I was not happy—"I" being Brandy Borne, a thirty-two-year-old divorced bottle-blonde who'd come running home to Mother (a.k.a. Vivian

Borne), home being the little Mississippi River town we call Serenity, Iowa. Well, everybody who lives here calls it Serenity, Iowa, but that includes us.

And someone else was not happy about being bothered: Sushi, my blind shih tzu, nestled behind my knees. The poochie was the consolation prize I'd slunk home with after the divorce—my bad, resulting from an indiscretion with an old boyfriend the weekend of my ten-year high school reunion. Jake, my thirteen-year-old son, lived with Roger in Chicago. But my ex and I had patched things up to the point where we were more than civil.

Civil toward Mother was not something Sushi and I felt right now, and we let out a low communal growl.

Still drumming, Mother chirped, "Uppie-uppie-uppie," as if I were still a child who might respond to that cheerfully delivered annoyance by reaching for, and tossing, a pillow.

I reached for and tossed a pillow.

Mother batted it away as if it were nothing more than an oversize snowflake, not missing a beat on the toy drum.

Croaking through the frog in my throat, I whined, "But I wanna sleep *iiiiiiin.*"

Monday was the only day we didn't have to work at our antiques store.

"Starving children in China want ice water," came her immediate if incoherent reply. "Up, up, *up*!"

"No!"

"Now, Brandy, we have places to go, things to do, and people to see."

I hate it when Mother says that, which is about every day, it seems.

"What time is it?" I groaned, sitting up. It was hard getting comfortable without a pillow. (I already knew the answer: eight o'clock; this was just more grousing.)

"Why . . . time to get *going*, dear," she replied sweetly, then strode out of the room (no longer banging her drum, thank goodness, but still marching to her own drummer . . . as always).

I had learned not to ask Mother about her agenda until I'd had a hot breakfast, just as she'd learned not to inflict it upon me until a cup of coffee had turned me semihuman.

I crawled out of bed, and stumbled off to the bathroom; Sushi, lucky her, stayed behind in a nest of blankets.

Shortly thereafter, refreshed, my shoulder-length hair squeaky clean (and actually brushed), I stepped into my DKNY jeans, tugged on a black V-neck cashmere sweater I'd snagged half-off last year, and headed barefoot downstairs. It's a two-story, turn-of-the-century home, or it had been before it got blown up (see *Antiques Roadkill*) and rebuilt from the original plans.

On the way to the dining room, I passed by our Christmas tree, in the front picture window, and shook my head. Not that it wasn't beautifully decorated—it very much was, this and every year a stunning collaborative Christmas vision courtesy of the Borne girls. We always trim our tree early, and this one had been up since early November—and I do mean *up* . . .

. . . hanging as it was by its base from the ceiling, limbs fanned out in drooping surrender.

Mother had seen this done in a downtown store last Christmas and, eager to find a unique way to display our tree, copied the idea. The tree was artificial, so keeping it well watered in an upside-down state was a nonissue. And it had been easy enough to decorate.

But that first night, the thing had come crashing to the floor during the wee hours, startling us from our beds, making us fear we had a burglar. We'd run downstairs, each with a baseball bat poised as if waiting for Santa to yell, "Play ball," and what to our wondering eyes should appear, but a pine tree that seemed to have dropped dead.

I'd just lowered my bat and eyed her, saying, "I'm not part of this. This is your mess."

"My culpa, dear. Strictly my culpa."

After that—about a third of the ornaments having shattered—I felt sure Mother would upright the poor thing, but she merely reinforced the hooks on the ceiling. I only prayed she wouldn't nail the presents to the ceiling, and as a precaution decided not to wrap anything breakable.

In the dining room, I plopped down at our Duncan Phyfe table, set as usual with vintage dinnerware we'd snagged at a flea market—beige, rimmed in 22-k gold, made by Triumph, and labeled "Hollywood." Very cool.

Even though Mother already owned enough dishes to feed those starving Chinese children their ice water, I hadn't squelched the buy because these were so impressively Art Deco in style, particularly the serving pieces.

While waiting to be served (the one thing not required of draftees is cooking their own food in the mess hall), I took the little capsule that Mother had placed on a small dessert dish for me, downing it with water from the glass—an antidepressant, which I'd felt necessary to use since coming home to live with her. (You may already understand my need for medication.)

Mother had a pill on her little plate, too, but hers was an antipsychotic for bipolar disorder, from which she'd suffered since her early twenties.

On the kitchen counter, next to a dual water/food dish that would soon be filled and placed on the floor, was a final dosage of medication. This was for Sushi—a syringe with insulin to be administered after the little diabetic's morning meal.

Now, before you go asking yourself, "Do I really want to spend any time with some mentally ill people and their sick dog?" I can assure you that we are all presently modulating within normal levels—at least, our idea of normal.

And, as for me being a nasty girl who ruined her marriage, I have cleaned up my life, and gone straight, straight to Iowa, anyway. So, go ahead, read on. What do you have to lose besides what you already spent on this? And if you got it free somehow, who are you to complain?

Mother, breezed in from the kitchen, carrying a tray of steaming bowls of oatmeal, hot coffee, and orange juice. She is in her seventies (where, exactly, no one really knows, not even me, and possibly not Mother, who has been lying about her age for so many years, she may have lost track).

This morning she sported her favorite emerald green velour slacks and top (her going-places-doing-things-seeing-people outfit), wavy silver hair pinned up, her Danish ancestry evident in the pale blue eyes, gently sloping nose, apple cheeks, and wide mouth. In addition to all these pluses was the minus of out-of-date oversize glasses whose lenses magnified her eyes in a somewhat bug-eye fashion.

Mother set the tray down, then placed one of the bowls of brown-sugar-sprinkled oatmeal before me, and I reached for the—

(**Mother to Brandy**: So sorry to interrupt, dear, but this is *a short* story, not one of our novels. Do move things along—we don't need every nuance.)

(**Brandy to Mother**: I was just setting the stage—you should know that, seasoned thespian that you are.)

(**Mother to Brandy**: Yes, thank you, dear, and I will assume you mean "seasoned" in the most flattering way. Now bring on the other players already.)

—spoon and dug in.

Besides antiquing, Mother is active in community theater, sometimes treading the boards, other times directing. Attending one of Mother's plays is always an experience, and I would share with you now an amusing anecdote about one of her many artistic triumphs, but there simply isn't time.

(**Mother to Brandy:** Sarcasm is not becoming to a young woman, dear, often causing premature aging. Now move it along.)

Once we had finished with our breakfast (satisfied, Mother?), I felt human enough to ask her, "All right, so what's on the docket for today?"

She patted her lips daintily with the cloth napkin, then folded it neatly on the table. "Dear, we are in dire need of Christmas stock."

She was right. We had recently expanded from a single rented booth in an antiques mall into our own business in a colorful old house located on the edge of the downtown. And Christmas sales could either make or break our expansion.

"Agreed," I said. "Any ideas?"

Which was a dumb question. *Of course* she had ideas—that's why I'd been rousted from my warm bed, sugarplums be darned.

"I have solid intel," she was saying, "that Bernie Watkins is considering selling his entire Yuletide collection—some of it dating back to the nineteen forties! Or so I'm told. I can't remember back that far, obviously."

I was nodding. If we could get to the old gent before anyone else, it would be quite a coup.

"And," Mother said, "I don't need to tell you that we need to act and act quickly."

"Right. Christmas is coming."

"No! Well, yes, it is coming. But we're bound

to have competition from you-know-who if he gets wind of this opportunity."

"Lyle Humphrey, you mean."

"Yes! He's the grinch who collects Christmas."

As long as I could remember (which was definitely *not* back to the 1940s), the Watkinses' house was *the* place to drive slowly by during the holiday season, because of the wondrous indoor/outdoor displays he had—Christmas lights everywhere, lit-up snowmen and other festive figures arrayed around the yard, Santa in his sleigh with reindeer balanced on the rooftop, and a decorated tree visible in seemingly every window of the house. When Bernie paid his December electric bill, it must have made a wonderful late Christmas present for the power and water company.

The Watkinses, Bernie and Velma, had both been grade-school teachers. Though childless in their marriage, they loved kids, as evidenced by their elaborate Yuletide displays, and Bernie had frequently played Santa Claus at local events. Christmas became an obsession with the couple, and word was they collected all sorts of holiday stuff. Then, after Velma passed, Bernie met his second wife, Emma, at one of those year-round Christmas shops, and the new couple never missed a beat where elaborate holiday displays were concerned.

The only difference was that Bernie and Emma had moved from Mulberry Street to just outside of town on River Road, a twisty two-lane hugging the banks of the Mississippi. As soon as word got out that their Christmas display was up and alit, the narrow highway became congested with crawling cars loaded with kids of all ages. Folks would enter Bernie's semicircle drive at one end, rubberneck, then slowly exit at the other end, and speed back to town past the endless caravan in the other lane.

Locals knew enough not to take River Road that time of year if they were in a hurry, and used the bypass instead. But some had no choice, like Bernie's next-door neighbor, Mr. Fusselman. Once, Mr. Fussy Man complained bitterly to the city council about the congestion, earning a collective hiss the following Sunday morning from the congregation of the Second Presbyterian Church. Nobody heard an anti-Christmas peep from Fusselman after that.

Mother had taken me to Bernie and Emma's one Christmas when I was just old enough to read. I had heard from another kid that there was a life-size Santa in the yard, holding a long list of the names of "good" kids, and that *his* name was on it! This kid was no prize, so I figured I was a shoo-in for the list—but when we got there, little Brandy hadn't made the cut! I tearfully blurted out my protest at this injustice, inspiring Mother to grab a pen from her purse, jump out, and—

(**Mother to Brandy**: Dear, please do stay on point. You weren't the first child to be disappointed at Christmastime, and you won't be the last. And, anyway, Mother took care of it, didn't she?)

When Emma died last year, I suppose it was

too hard (and sad) for Bernie to carry on alone with the Christmas decorating, and of course he wasn't getting any younger himself. So it made sense that he might now want to unburden himself of his decorations and collectibles.

Still in a hot oatmeal afterglow, I asked Mother, "So, does Bernie know we're coming?"

Another stupid question. Mother was strictly a drop-by.

"No, Bernie adores a good surprise. And whose face doesn't blossom into a smile when they answer the doorbell and see that Vivian Borne has come to call?"

"Most of the population of Serenity?"

"Tish tosh," she said. Is that a saying? Does or did anybody else ever say that? Anyway, she rose from the table. "Dress warm, dear. It's beginning to snow."

Sushi could tell whenever we were leaving, even though we did our best not to utter certain words, including "go" and "car." And yet there she was, dancing at my feet.

"All right." I smiled, scooping up the little devil. "You can go in the car, too."

And of course the word "car" coupled with "go" turned her into a wriggling furry mass of joy-to-her-world.

Soon we were trundling off in our heavy coats, out through a dusting of snowfall to my gently dented Buick, me behind the wheel, coaxing the car to life, Mother riding shotgun with Sushi on her lap. Then we were headed to downtown, a grid of five blocks nestled on the banks of the Muddy Miss, with everything a little

Iowa burg like ours could need. (Notice I didn't say "want.")

Then we were tooling along River Road, the brightness of the sudden appearance of the sun glancing off the glistening water and the gathering snow along the roadside, a lovely sight that made me squint like a mole.

Mother sneezed.

Mother sneezed again.

She gave me a look. "You didn't say 'Bless you.' "

"That's because you didn't say 'Excuse me.' "

"Why should I do that?"

"Because *you're* the one disturbing the peace."

"Well," she sniffed, "the 'excuse me' is implied."

"Ditto the 'bless you.' "

That was the extent of our conversation on the drive out to Bernie's place, preoccupied as we both were, knowing our mission depended on beating Lyle Humphrey to the punch.

Lyle was a wealthy collector who had a penchant for Christmas collectibles. Awhile back at an auction, he and Mother had tangled over a plaster bank, about six inches high, of a slumbering Santa in a comfy chair.

Mother had bid $100, top dollar for the piece and a rare preemptive bid from her; but Humphrey had shut her down by going $200.

"Double book!" she had shouted at him in the parking lot. "Double book!"

Lyle had a round baby face, rounded shoulders, and rounder tummy; though it was summer, he had worn a three-piece suit. "You're looking lovely today, Lillian."

"That's *Vivian*!"

"Is it?"

"You're a horrible little man!"

He'd winced momentarily, as if his feelings were hurt, then smiled smugly. "Perhaps I am, but nothing was stopping you from bidding again. If a person really wants something, a person goes after it."

But Lyle had known we—and few of those he went up against in auctions—could never stand up to his kind of money.

Soon I was swinging the Buick into the semicircle drive of Bernie's place. I pulled the car up in front and we got out, Mother handing Sushi over to me. Without cover of darkness and glitz of Christmas lights, Serenity's favorite seasonal sight looked a trifle shabby. The white ranch-style home was in need of some TLC by way of fresh paint and roof shingles, and the yard didn't seem ready for winter, not having gotten over autumn yet, judging by the clumpy scatterings of leaves.

As we approached the open cement porch, I pointed to where several newspapers had piled up. "Maybe Bernie's on vacation. Doesn't look like he's been home for a while."

Mother nodded in agreement.

I was turning to go, but Mother pressed on, climbing the few steps to the front door, then brazenly tried to open it, but it was locked, thank goodness.

"Mother! What would you have done if that was open? Marched right in?"

She shrugged. "Not 'march' exactly. Moot point now, dear."

"Maybe he has an answering machine you can leave a message on. In the meantime, let's head back and regroup. There *have* to be other sources for Christmas collectibles."

Mother, having returned to my side, replied, "I'm not ready to leave just yet, dear."

And before I could ask her why not, she headed over to a nearby outbuilding, a large metal and poured cement prefabricated affair with a normal door next to a double garage-style door.

"What are you *doing*, Mother?"

Another silly question, not rating an answer.

"Let's not *break-and-enter*, Mother!"

With a half-turn of the head, as if responding to me was barely worth it (not a bad estimation, actually), she said, "It's not breaking and entering, dear, when the door is unlocked!"

The door was unlocked.

Only the gray winter sky heard my groan, because Mother had already disappeared inside.

I stood there like a female snowman for a few seconds, white stuff collecting in my hair like dandruff, shrugged, then followed her bad example. She was probably right. If you didn't break anything, how could it be breaking and entering?

I entered.

It wasn't exactly warm in the cement-floored building—my breath still smoking—but this was an improvement over standing outside, where the snow was coming down increasingly harder.

I dusted the stuff off of Sushi, then gazed around in amazement, my mouth dropping like a trapdoor. The high-ceilinged building was packed with antiques and collectibles, with rows of jammed shelving and little pathways leading from one delight to another, and all of it was Christmas oriented, evenly divided between Nativity-scene religiosity and Santa Claus commercialism.

A middle section had heavy cardboard standees dating to the thirties and forties with famous movie stars of the day, many in Santa outfits, peddling everything from pop to cigarettes. You could get your Camels and Lucky Strikes in some pretty festive cartons, back in the day.

From somewhere toward the rear, Mother called out, "*Dear!* You simply *must* see this! It's exactly what we need to dress the store up and attract more business!"

Following her slightly echoing voice, I was led to the sight of her standing by an old Victorian-style sleigh, which on closer examination appeared to be of a considerable vintage. Beautifully restored and of mahogany wood, it had a black lacquered chaise, iron rudders, and seated four on two separate red velvet–buttoned covered benches. It was adorable.

I turned eagerly to Mother. "Do you think Bernie would let us borrow it?"

"Why not *buy* it? He's getting rid of everything."

"This piece could be a hundred years old or more. I don't think we can afford it, and it wouldn't be for resale . . . strictly decorative, right?"

She smiled slyly. "I'm sure I can convince the old boy to either loan it or give it to us for a song. Make that a carol."

Where men of a certain age were concerned, Mother had many convincing ways: cajoling, bribing, and some you don't want to know about. Like blackmail. Did I type that out loud?

Setting Soosh down on the back bench and commanding her to "stay" (I batted about .500 on that one), I circled the sleigh, visualizing it in the front of our store, the center of a fabulous display, or even out in the yard, strung with lights.

Sushi was barking.

Mother frowned. "Now, what's wrong with *her*? Doesn't she have the Christmas spirit?"

"She only gets the Christmas spirit when I put those bones in her stocking. Something's got her wired up."

The little fur ball had her front legs down on the seat, little butt twitching in the air, like the Jeep in a Popeye cartoon.

"What is it, girl?" I asked.

The barking became earsplitting, echoing off the cement.

I looked where she seemed to be trying to draw my attention; the shape of a blanket on the floor of the sleigh, between the benches, was vaguely human.

"Soosh, that's nothing. That's just a blanket."

Mother said dismissively, "She's just sniffing the owner's scent."

But Sushi pawed at the blanket, and one corner slipped back . . .

. . . revealing a gray wool cap and wisps of silver hair matted with blood.

The little dog had sniffed the owner's scent, all right.

Chapter Two

You Sleigh Me

Sheriff Rudder arrived about ten minutes after Mother placed the 911 call on her cell—Bernie's property being outside the city limits, making this the sheriff's jurisdiction.

Rudder was a tall, burly man who reminded me somewhat of John Wayne, if I closed my eyes till they blurred a little. He had a fairly gruff demeanor, unless that was just how he behaved around Mother and me. (Yes, we'd had a few past run-ins with the sheriff—or mostly Mother had.)

The light blue car had SHERIFF, COUNTY OF SERENITY inscribed in black on its driver's-side and passenger doors. A young deputy was driving, and Rudder got out on the rider's side.

"That's the building right over there," Mother told him, pointing.

Rudder said nothing, blowing right by us.

Mother started to follow him, but at the sound of her boots crunching snow, he turned and gave her a stern "stop" motion with one hand, like a surly crossing guard to a precocious grade-school kid. She returned to my side, swinging her arms, mildly disgruntled.

"Who's solved more murders around here?" she asked the air. "Him or me?"

The air didn't reply, but I did. "Maybe you shouldn't bring that up."

"Well . . . all right."

"And, anyway, I helped."

We had a running argument over who was Holmes and who was Watson. We weren't sure who Sushi was. Mrs. Hudson?

After a little while, the sheriff came out, speaking on his cell, and we heard him ask for an ambulance and the coroner.

Then finally he joined Mother and me, as we stood shivering by our Buick. I had placed Sushi inside my buttoned-up coat, her little head poking out, like a hairy goiter.

"*You* found Mr. Watkins?" Rudder asked Mother brusquely.

"Well, if you want to be technical," she said, "it was Sushi who discovered the poor man. Our little dog? But I don't suppose you can take her statement."

Was she being facetious? Don't ask me.

But Rudder thought she was, and his face grew ruddier. "Why were you here, Vivian?"

"Well, my dear man," Mother replied, slipping into the faux British accent she unconsciously assumed to sound more important, "Brandy and I had come to see Bernie about buying some of his Christmas collectibles for our shop. Perhaps you're not aware that we recently moved from the mall to—"

"What time was that?" Rudder interrupted.

Mother put a hand to her chin. "Well, now, we had finished our breakfast about nine. And the drive out here took about seventeen, eighteen . . ."—she checked her wristwatch—". . . possibly nineteen—"

"Best guess," he cut in again.

Mother bristled, pulling herself up. "Sheriff Rudder, guesswork may be fine for the constabulary. But *not* for Vivian Borne! After all, my daughter and I do not wish to be considered suspects in this matter. Murder. Matter."

"Whether it's a 'matter' or a 'murder' hasn't been established yet, Vivian."

Mother smirked. "Let's not be coy, Sheriff—it's obvious poor Bernie had been hit on the head with something heavy enough to cave in his skull."

Yes, while I was waiting outside for the sheriff to arrive, Mother had gone back into the building to examine the body and do a quick search for clues.

Rudder waggled a finger in Mother's face. "If you've compromised the crime scene, Vivian, there'll be hell to pay!"

"That kind of language, Sheriff, at this festive, sacred time of year, is simply not—"

"Sit in your car!" A thick forefinger pointed to my Buick. "*Both* of you—until I say otherwise."

Mother smiled sweetly. "May I make one small observation?"

"Can I stop you?"

"This ungracious, unprofessional attitude of yours—it wouldn't have anything to do with the unfortunate happenings the last time I was a visitor in your lockup, would it?"

(Sorry, no time to go into Mother's latest stint in the county hoosegow. Suffice it to say she's a fairly regular guest.)

"In the car!" Rudder shouted. "Now!"

"There's no need to be rude," Mother said ambiguously, as I was at the time stuffing her into the Buick.

I got in, too, behind the wheel. My head and Sushi's looked at her from my coat.

"No need to get physical, dear," she huffed, dusting off the snow as if looking to see if her dignity was under there.

"Let's not get on the sheriff's bad side any more than we already are, Mother—we may need him." And I started the engine to get us warm. "Not that I recall ever *seeing* his good side."

"Still, he may be useful at that. Excellent point, dear."

Our attention was drawn to the yellow paramedic truck that had just pulled up, two men in orange suits jumping from the cab, the sheriff striding toward them.

A gray sedan followed, conveying the coroner, and Mother watched intently as a short, heavyset, bespectacled man climbed out, carrying a black medical bag, snow riding the wreath of hair around his bald pate like bad makeup at the local playhouse. And, believe me, it can be pretty bad.

"Oh, dear," Mother sighed. "Hector's gained weight. On the positive side, that means he must be in love again."

"Why in love?"

"I know Hector, dear. His passion is good cooking. To him, a bedroom is just for sleeping."

I had no more questions on this subject, wishing no further answers.

Then the sheriff, paramedics, and coroner disappeared into the prefab building.

Sushi, now overheated, was wiggling/wriggling to get out of my coat. I withdrew the pooch, as if she'd been filed away, and was about to hand her over to Mother when a battered red truck clunked into the drive, bounced up behind the other vehicles, and thudded to an abrupt stop.

The two people in the truck, a man at the wheel with a woman riding, had alarmed expressions that I suspected had little to do with the perils of travel in that truck.

"Do you know them?" I asked.

Yet another stupid question: Mother knew everybody in Serenity.

"Bernie's stepdaughter and stepson," Mother said, adding excitedly, "They must not know about Bernie!"

"That's terrible," I said, just as Mother was saying, "That's wonderful." As I goggled at her, she said, "Dear, this is a rare opportunity to see their reaction to the news! They're potential suspects, you know."

And before I could stop her—it should, obviously, be the sheriff to inform them of the tragedy—Mother was out of the car and heading over to the pair, her boots kicking up new-fallen snow.

I folded my arms, wanting nothing to do with this. Or anyway, I did so after powering down my window to hear what went on.

The stepdaughter, who had hopped out of the truck's passenger side (her brother was still behind the wheel), asked Mother, "What's happened here? Is Bernie all right?"

Bernie. Not "Dad."

She was a hard-living forty, thin, with outdated short permed brown hair. She wore a black Harley jacket and skin-tight jeans and motorcycle boots.

Her brother, having now joined her, proved shorter than his sister, but wider. He wore a baseball cap, brim pulled low over his face, and jeans, an orange-and-brown hunting jacket straining at a burly upper torso.

Mother said, "My dears . . . I'm afraid I have simply terrible news. Your father—that is, your *stepfather*—has passed on."

"Oh, no," the sister said, fingers flying to her lips.

The brother was frowning, like a really dumb high school kid at the moment he realizes he won't be passing geometry. "You mean he's dead?"

"I'm afraid so," Mother said, hamming up the sympathy, adding, "But I fear it's even worse than that."

She was making them ask!

The brother asked, "What's worse than dead?"

"Excellent question," she said. "He's been murdered."

The "m" word had just passed her lips when the door to the building opened, and Rudder, stepping out, caught sight of Mother talking to the pair, after which he let out what I might best describe as a war whoop as he ran forward. Fortunately, he did not have an Indian battle axe handy.

"Vivian Borne!" Rudder shouted. "Get *back* in your car—and get *out* of here."

Mother looked hurt, the sister, startled, the brother confused.

The sheriff gestured forcefully to the highway. *"Now!"*

"Leave the crime scene? Without making a statement?" She turned to the brother and sister for support. "I found the body in the antique sleigh. Or anyway, my daughter's dog did. Is it really responsible police procedure to send me away?"

Rudder could only have turned a deeper shade of red if he were Elmer Fudd in a Technicolor cartoon from 1945. "Vivian! Goddamnit!"

"Language, Sheriff! I presume I should not leave town."

"Oh, leave town. Please! By all means, leave town!"

I powered up my window, and clicked on my seat belt.

I was pretty sure we were leaving.

But not town.

Chapter Three

It's Beginning to Look a Lot Like Murder

This is Vivian taking the reins, dears, because after we had returned to our domicile, Brandy went straight back up to bed—so, for the nonce, she is no help either as detective or as narrator!

But I ask you, how could the girl sleep after what had just happened? Is she really that cold-blooded? Or perhaps narcoleptic? Topics for discussion at a later date.

For now, I grabbed my coat and purse again, and after borrowing Brandy's oh-so-warm new UGG boots, I headed out into the gently falling snow to catch a ride downtown. For reasons too numerous and unfair to go into, I have been deprived of my driver's license. So when Brandy is not available as my chauffeur, I make use of a certain public conveyance—a gas-converted trolley car, provided free by the downtown merchants, which makes regular stops around Serenity, including one a mere block away from the Borne hacienda.

Once again, Maynard Kirby was behind the wheel, having returned to work after his wife lost their latest lottery winnings. I greeted him warmly, and he reciprocated.

My dears, I would love to regale you with some wonderfully witty stories about the trolley passengers—especially tales about the midget and the monkey (two separate incidents); but time is of the essence, as is word count, since both Brandy and our New York editor have made the unwise decision to limit my participation as coauthor. They claim that, unbridled, I would contribute (to quote our editor) "enough excessive discursive material to require decimating a forest to provide the paper." I put it to you: have I gotten off the track? No—I got *on* the trolley, and I even resisted sharing the midget and monkey stories with you.

But I digress.

Soon I was disembarking in front of the Riverview Restaurant, where I knew the Romeos (Retired Old Men Eating Out) would be holding court, consuming the kind of fattening comfort-food lunch that their wives wouldn't cook for them anymore, due to health concerns. (Some of the men were widowers, but obviously *their* wives weren't cooking for them anymore, either.)

I would also love to give you a description of the quaint, riverboat-themed restaurant on the first floor of a restored Victorian building, but I can't, due to this restricted format. Wait a minute—I just did! And without going on and on and on about it. Perhaps sometimes less *is* more.

As usual, the Romeos were at their customary round table in back, which could seat six, though three of the chairs were empty today, probably due to the cold and flu season, not to mention the Grim Reaper, who had claimed a few of their members this year.

Normally, the Romeos were a closed boys' club, but I was an exception, sort of the Shirley MacLaine to their Rat Pack. I was especially welcome if I brought along some juicy tidbit of news to pass around the table, to season their meals. These old codgers were worse gossips than any of my lady friends. Granted, they were more subtle about it—that is, they kept their voices down.

Unfortunately, the gents had already been served the blue plate special (mashed potatoes, green peas, and meatloaf), which meant I'd have to watch them eat—never a pretty sight, as more food seemed to go on their faces than within. Add to that the clacking of plates, and I don't mean dishes (I mean dentures) (in case you weren't following).

But again I digress.

I gave the trio my best Mae West, "Hell-*low*, boy-*ez*."

Harold said, " 'lo Viv, what's new, my little chickadee?" The latter might have been amusing had Harold been able to do a passable W. C. Fields impression, but though the ex–army captain resembled the older Bob Hope, he wasn't nearly as funny.

I laughed anyway. That's what a female does when a man thinks he's being clever. Anyway, it's what I do, and it's served me well.

After Harold's wife died, he'd asked me out several times, and hinted from the start at matrimony; but I broke it off after a few weeks because he barked orders at me. Actually, he barked *everything* at me—Sushi's yapping can get on my nerves, too, but this was more like a rabid bulldog. Seems you can take the man out of the army, but not the army out of the man, and Vivian Borne doesn't take orders from *anybody*.

"Vivian!" Vern blurted pleasantly. "Come and join us!" The retired chiropractor looked vaguely like Clark Gable, minus the ears sticking out.

Vern, too, had wanted to marry me, but I threw cold water on his ardor, which coincidentally was what the fire department had also had to do at his place of business when the building spontaneously combusted due to the stacks of outdated magazines piling up in his waiting room. What a cheapskate! Which was another reason to say fiddle dee dee to Vern and his intentions.

The third gentleman, Wendell, was a former Mississippi River tugboat pilot, and a ringer for Leo Gorcey (you youngsters can check with the good folks at Wikipedia for information on the gifted thespian who brought Slip Mahoney to life—or you could just Google the Dead End Kids).

As for Wendell's husband potential, the point was moot. First of all, Wendell was not available. But even if he were, I would take a pass, because despite his Old Spice aftershave, the bouquet of fish seemed always to cling to him. He was still hanging out on the river after he'd been forced to retire when his tugboat rammed the *Delta Queen* paddleboat, whose calliope at that very moment had been playing "Bim Bam Boom."

Wendell gestured to the vacant chair next to him, and, since my nose was stopped up with a seasonal cold, what the hey, I just plopped myself down.

Pretty, dark-haired Susan, one of the best waitresses in town, had seen me come in, and efficiently placed a cup of java before me, just the way I like it: one sugar, two creams.

Susan and I exchanged smiles. She knew I would soon have these old boys eating out of my hand. So to speak.

"Well," I said, settling in, "guess where I've been this morning?"

They all looked at me, though no one stopped shoveling chow-filled spoons into their open maws to risk a guess.

I went on: "I just came from Bernie Watkins's place."

The men paused, forks frozen in midair—did they have competition for the favors of Vivian Borne by way of Bernard Watkins?

No, they didn't, and I explained why. "Poor Bernie's been murdered."

Harold began to choke on his meatloaf, the ex–army captain never having learned the first rule of battle: do not have a mouthful of food during Vivian Borne's opening salvo.

"Good Lord," gasped Wendell. "Not another murder! How many does that make in this town, over the last couple years?"

I said, "Who's counting?"

Vern asked, "How did you know he'd been murdered, Viv?"

The chiro obviously assumed I'd heard about Bernie's murder and had gone out there to offer my services as an amateur sleuth. After all, I had (with some assistance from Brandy) solved all of those murders Wendell referred to. And yet the local police viewed me as a nuisance!

"Yeah, Vivian," Harold said. "How did you hear that? You buy yourself a police scanner or something?"

Excellent idea!

Pausing for effect, I took a dainty sip of my coffee, little finger extended, then said nonchalantly, "Why, I didn't hear it anywhere, dear—'twas I who found the body."

You might think that was a little arch, but with my understated line reading, it played just fine. They were all ears and eyes—albeit ears that could use some trimming of unnecessary hair, and eyes that were bloodshot and rheumy.

Then I regaled my audience with the gory details, omitting only Brandy's and Sushi's presence, for conciseness and word count.

(**Brandy to Mother**: Bull-hockey. You just wanted to hog all the glory in front of the old boys. And, by the way? That calliope was playing "Come To Me My Melancholy Baby," *not* "Bim Bam Boom"—which I refuse to believe is a real song.)

(**Mother to Brandy**: The calliope was *too* playing "Bim Bam Boom"! And it *is* a real song, by the El Dorados, a doo-wop group from the 1950s. Look it up, dear.)

(**Brandy to Mother**: I *did* look it up. According to the "good folks at Wikipedia," the tune was called "At My Back Door," not "Bim Bam Boom.")

(**Mother to Brandy**: That's a technicality! The *chorus* goes "bim bam boom," which is how all of us who loved the tune remember it. Funny how it rarely turns up on oldies radio. . . .)

(**Editor to Vivian and Brandy**: Ladies, this squabbling must stop—you're looking foolish and unprofessional. Get back on point—don't you have a murder to solve? Or would you like to have your short-story contract cancelled?)

(**Vivian to Editor**: What about our novels?)

(**Editor to Vivian**: Perhaps those, as well.)

(**Vivian to Editor**: We'll behave.)

(**Brandy to Editor**: Ditto.)

Harold, his coughing fit curtailed, windpipe cleared, grunted, "I bet those no-good stepkids of his killed ol' Bernie."

"Oh?" I said, liking the direction this was going.

He nodded. "After Emma died, they only came back to town to get their hands on his money."

Wendell said, "Christmas around Serenity won't be the same without Bernie's display."

"He was already planning not to decorate this year," I said. Then I turned back to Harold. "Those stepchildren—where *was* their home before moving here?"

Harold shrugged. "Burlington, I think."

Wendell said, "Just not the same, Christmas in Serenity."

Vern nodded. "Neither one of those two lowlifes could hold onto a job *or* a marriage for very long."

"Is that why they moved up here from Burlington?"

After a sip (more like a slurp) of coffee, Vern continued. "Maybe partly. But after Emma's funeral, they moved in with Bernie—supposedly to take care of him in his golden years."

Wendell said, "Just not the same."

I asked, "Did they? Take care of him?"

"Naw," Vern said. "Wasn't long before he tossed them out on their collective behind."

Harold snorted. "Seems the pair ran up a whole mess of bills Bernie had to cover."

Wendell said, "A tradition, driving out there and seeing all those decorations. Not the same."

I asked, "So where are they staying now?"

"Rivercrest Apartments, I think," Vern said, adding, "The female anyway—don't know about that bum."

"Why a 'bum'?"

"Not the same," Wendell said. He looked a little teary eyed.

"Well," Vern said, drawing the word out, "the brother—Bo-Bo? Served time down in Fort Madison."

That perked my interest. "What was the charge?"

"Assault and battery. Some bar fight down there. Hurt somebody real bad. Fool was damn lucky it wasn't manslaughter."

"That's what I heard," Harold said, nodding. "And his sister, that loose gal Tanya? Not much better than Bo-Bo." He glanced around at his fellow Romeos. "Didn't I see her name in the paper for DUI?"

Nods all around the table, except for me, since I'd dropped the *Serenity Sentinel* after that mean-spirited review of my lead performance in *Everybody Loves Opal.* A prophet is never appreciated in her hometown.

I asked them collectively, "What sort of an estate do you suppose Bernie has?"

The trio looked at each other, exchanging shrugs.

Harold offered, "Well, he was a retired teacher, of course. And I never heard of him having inherited money from any relative or anything. There *is* the house, and about an acre of land."

Vern added, "*And* all those Christmas collectibles and antiques, acquired over, oh, four or five decades. That could be worth more than the property."

Wendell said, "Won't be the same at Christmastime."

"Yes, yes," I said impatiently, but then Wendell surprised me, saying, "You know, Bernie didn't want any of his Christmas things going to those two wastes of skin."

I frowned. "You know this for a fact, Wendell?"

"Oh, yes. Bernie and me were pals. We had coffee once a month or so. He told me he planned on changing his will so the antiques would go to a museum, where they'd be appreciated. There's a Christmas museum in Pella that he was talking to."

"You suppose Bernie's will reflected that?"

Wendell shrugged. "That I don't know. But I do know who his lawyer was, if that helps."

It did.

I thanked the boys for my coffee—the dears always picked up my check—gathered my coat and purse, and headed out into the pleasantly wintery afternoon.

A few blocks away, on Main Street, was the Laurel Building, an eight-story Art Deco edifice whose upper floors once housed the thriving practice of Wayne Ekhardt, one of the Midwest's most famous criminal lawyers. In a town the size of Serenity, however, Ekhardt and his firm had needed to take on all other sorts of legal work, too. As Wendell had said, Ekhardt had been Bernie's lawyer.

And he was mine.

Ekhardt's fame began in the 1950s when he got a woman off scot-free for shooting her abusive husband in self-defense. In the back. Five times. For a good while after that, husbands around here really went out of their way to be especially nice to their better halves.

Wayne, now approaching a spry ninety, was semi-semi-retired, retaining only a few valued clients, whom he saw by appointment only (on Wednesdays) in the small office he retained on the top floor.

I took the elevator up there, then stepped off into a world that hadn't changed since I was in diapers (and I will truck with no smart comments about Depends). The floor's tiny black-and-white tiles, marble gray walls, pebble-glass-and-wood office doors, and even Deco water fountain dated at least to the 1930s.

Wayne's office was at the end of the long hallway, a corner room with a magnificent view of the river, which unfortunately he could little appreciate these days, due to his cataracts.

This being Monday, the door was locked, but that didn't stop *Vivian Borne* from entering by way of one of Wayne's extra keys, borrowed from his desk for just such an occasion. Soon I was entering what could have been the professional digs of Philip Marlowe or Mike Hammer, albeit without an outer desk for a sexy secretary to sit behind, or maybe on, filing her nails and showing off her gams.

Zeroing in on an old wooden file cabinet, I rifled through it, withdrew the manila folder labeled BERNIE WATKINS, copied the contents at a nearby Xerox machine, then put the file back.

Quick as Old Saint Nick going up a chimney,

I put the copies in my purse, and dashed away, dashed away, dashed away out of there!

No need to make Sheriff Rudder's Christmas wish come true and provide him cause to book me into one of his "suites" to greet the New Year behind bars.

plain, within reach of the river's crest during spring flooding, and as such, the inhabitants were mostly low-income renters who didn't mind getting their stuff water damaged, or anyway couldn't afford to mind. But Rivercrest was nonetheless a decent-looking modern apartment complex.

I pulled the Buick into the parking lot, wondering which of the three three-story buildings was Tanya and Bo-Bo's. My eyes lingered over a red truck—*the* red truck.

A mailbox inside Building Two led me up to the second floor.

Frankly, I was hoping that neither bro nor sis would be home, and that they had remained at their stepfather's, or were otherwise engaged in preliminary funeral arrangements.

But Tanya answered my knock, wearing the same clothes as this morning, and not at all in mourning—no red eyes, no puffy face. Just a sullen expression, her eyes saying, "Yeah?" Her mouth didn't bother to say anything.

"Ah, hi," I said chirpily. "I'm Brandy Borne."

"You was at the house," she said flatly.

"Yes. Could I come in?"

She shrugged, said, "Knock yourself out," then turned her back on me and wandered away, but left the door open.

I stepped into a messy living room, littered with beer cans and empty pizza boxes. It was what happened when a high school kid's parents were away, only no high school kids or parents lived here.

Bo-Bo rose from a tattered couch like the hockey mask guy in the horror movies after you thought you killed him. "Who the hell's that?" He was minus the hunting jacket and baseball cap, but otherwise dressed as before—jeans, sweatshirt.

Tanya screwed her face up. Whether that meant she was thinking or about to spit, I couldn't tell you. "Says her name is Brandy something—she was with that ding-a-ling woman who told us about Bernie."

I said, "That's my mother."

Bo-Bo snorted. "You oughta stick that old broad in a nuthouse. She's looney tunes—everybody in town says so."

I laughed once. "Oh, well, what can you do? You can choose your friends but not your relatives."

(**Mother to Brandy**: How sharper than a serpent's tongue it is to have a thankless child!)

(**Brandy to Mother**: Mother, I wasn't being thank-less . . . I was playing them for information. And it's "tooth," not "tongue.")

(**Mother to Brandy**: Oh! Good strategy, dear. Carry on. I forgive you for whatever disparaging thing you might say about me, if it helps our inquiry.)

I told the pair, "That's why I'm here—to apologize for her wack-a-doodle behavior. I brought a peace offering."

And I handed Tanya the covered plate of cookies.

She accepted it, saying, "Well, I *guess* it's all right. Relatives *can* be a pain, all right."

Bo-Bo eyed me suspiciously. "Okay, so that's why you're here, 'cause of that fruitcake."

Tanya said, "It's cookies, not a fruitcake . . . oh. I see what you mean."

Bo-Bo frowned, shook his head, then said, "But what the hell were you two doin' out at *Bernie's*?"

I gave him a smile that was at least as sweet as those cookies. "We were hoping Bernie might sell us some of his collectibles. We have an antiques shop in town. But now that he's celebrating Christmas upstairs"—I pointed to the ceiling—"I supposed we should ask you."

Bo-Bo looked upward, frowning, perhaps thinking I meant the upstairs neighbors.

"Yes," Tanya said brightly, then put on a sad face. "But maybe it *is* a little soon to be thinking about that."

"Hell it is," Bo-Bo said, approaching me. "You're welcome to make an offer."

"An offer?"

"Yeah. But you'll have to beat that other guy's prices."

"Whose prices?"

"Oddball named Lyle Humphrey—know him?"

I nodded. Mother had been right about the need to act fast where our wealthy collector "friend" was concerned.

"I'll get what he gave us." Bo-Bo left the

room, came back, and handed me a computer printout with three columns, and the headings: ITEM, ESTIMATED WORTH, OFFER. I could tell at a glance that the last two columns were way below market value. Lyle may have been wealthy, but he sure wasn't generous.

I asked, "When did he give this to you?"

Tanya said, "About an hour ago."

"What?"

"Yeah, he said he done an appraisal for Bernie, and when he heard on the news about what happened, he made this list up for us."

"That's a little cold."

Bo-Bo sneered at me. "Well, *you're* here asking, aren't you? Early bird gets the worm."

"Fair enough," I said, and held up the sheet. "May I keep this? I can work from it so we can give you a better offer."

"Sure thing, honey," Tanya said. "We got another copy."

"Thanks." I turned to go, then looked back at them. "By the way, when did you see your stepfather last?"

Tanya and Bo-Bo exchanged glances before she answered. "About a week ago. We tried calling him yesterday and didn't get an answer. Tried again this morning, and finally went out to see if the old fella was okay."

Bo-Bo shrugged. "And, of course, he wasn't."

I nodded. "I'll be in touch. Enjoy the cookies."

Part of me wished I'd sprinkled them with

chocolate-flavored Ex-Lax shavings. But that wouldn't have been in the Christmas spirit, would it? Though it would have been a gift that kept on giving.

Chapter Five

Makin' a List

It was late afternoon by the time I returned home to find that my new UGGs had mysteriously reappeared in the foyer. Some mysteries just can't be solved, can they . . . *Mother?*

Speaking of whom, I found La Diva Borne seated at the dining-room table, hunkered over a spread of official-looking papers.

"How did it go, dear?" she asked.

Sitting down, I recounted my conversation with Tanya and Bo-Bo, then handed her the printout of the prices offered them by Lyle Humphrey.

"That fits in interestingly with what I've found," Mother mused, eyes narrowing to normal size behind the large lenses as she looked the printout over. "I think our old bidding rival Lyle Humphrey intends to dupe the pair."

"Couldn't happen to a nicer couple." I gestured toward the papers before her. "What are those?"

"Among other things, a copy of a new will Wayne had prepared for Bernie, which would have cut Tanya and Bo-Bo out."

"*Would* have? You're saying it's not signed?"

"That's right, dear."

"Talk about a motive for murder," I said. "Can an unsigned will be legal? It *was* Bernie's intention, after all."

Mother shook her head. "Not if there is a signed one—of which Tanya and Bo-Bo *are* the beneficiaries. Of course, we don't know that they were aware of this new document."

Few lawyers knew more about wills than Mother, who had done her studying on the subject by reading Agatha Christie.

I nodded toward the thing. "Where'd you get it?"

Mother smiled slyly. "Sometimes ignorance is not only bliss, but a self-protective posture."

"You mean, what I don't know won't hurt me."

"On the nose, dear."

"Like I can't figure out that you broke into Mr. Ekhardt's office with that pass key you pilfered from his desk when he fell asleep the last time we met with him."

Mother frowned. "Now you've just made yourself an accessory after the fact. Happy?"

"You've gotten me into worse trouble." (See *any* of our books.)

I picked up the copy of the new will and leafed

through it, noting that—along with several monetary bequeaths to various charities—a museum in Pella had been designated to get Bernie's collectibles and antiques. Of course, now everything would go to his stepdaughter and stepson.

Attached to the back of the will was another printout of an antiques appraisal, but this time with only two columns: one listing the antiques, the other their current worth—more in line with reality. It was dated five days ago—last Wednesday.

"Hey, it's Humphrey again," I said. "This seems to be the source of the inventory list he gave Bo-Bo and Tanya."

"I'm sure it is. According to documents in the file, Bernie hired Lyle to make an appraisal of his collection, as a formality for tax and various legal purposes in leaving his things to the museum."

I returned the papers to Mother, then went into the kitchen to warm up our dinner—leftover lasagne (always better the second day).

When I returned to set the table, Mother was making a closer comparison of the will's inventory with Tanya and Bo-Bo's printout.

She handed the documents to me. "Dear, take a gander at these. See if you find something suggestive, as Hercule Poirot might say."

I sat and studied them. "They match up almost perfectly. Almost. There's one item on the earlier list that isn't on the recent one. Did Bo-Bo and Tanya doctor their list for some reason?

They said they had two copies, so maybe Mr. Humphrey gave them a computer file and they edited it. Why, I can't imagine."

Mother's eyes flared, like somebody had thrown a log on the fire. "Dear, after we eat, why don't we drop in on our old friend Lyle Humphrey, for a little clarification."

"Remember that parking lot hissy fit of yours, after that auction? He won't exactly be thrilled to see us."

"Nonsense. He's an old veteran of the bidding wars, and knows how high emotions can run." She was paging through again. "Dear, I need to study these documents more closely, so you'll have time to—"

"Don't tell me—frost some Christmas cookies to take him as a peace-on-earth offering."

Lyle Humphrey lived on East Hill, a once ritzy part of Serenity first settled by bankers, lumber mill barons, and pearl button factory owners, who built their fabulous mansions overlooking the Mississippi. Some very rich folks still live there, though it's more of a mix now, and not all of the homes have been well maintained. Lyle's home fell somewhere in the upper reaches of that spectrum.

I didn't know Lyle all that well, despite our occasional encounters at area auctions; but, of course, Mother knew him better, and filled me in on the way over.

"I would say Lyle is a man of perhaps fifty-five or -six or -seven or -eight," she said.

"A man in his fifties, then."

"Isn't that what I said, dear? He was always something of a momma's boy, and I don't think he ventures out of the family manse very often for anything other than his antiquing quests."

"So he doesn't work or anything?"

"Oh, no, dear. He had a substantial inheritance. I've been meaning to arrange a viewing of what I understand are considerably impressive displays of his various collecting passions. But, lately, after our auction run-ins . . ."

"You called him a 'horrible little man,' remember?"

"Yes, but I meant that only in a positive sense. Everyone can benefit from a soupçon of constructive criticism."

"Really? Then why did we drop the *Serenity Sentinel*?"

"Pish posh," Mother said.

Is that a thing? Pish posh? Somebody please write in and tell me.

I pulled the Buick into the drive of the imposing Renaissance Revival mansion, parking beneath a covered portico. Mother and I got out, me lugging Sushi under my coat (she'd thrown a mini-fit when we started to leave again) (single mothers spoil their children), Mother carrying the plate of cookies.

We stood for a moment in the frosty air, admiring the cube-shaped structure silhouetted against a night sky, admiring too its smooth stone walls, wide eaves, and ornately trimmed windows buttressed by columns, which gave the old place a palatial feel. We were visiting Serenity antiquing royalty.

Mother's eyes shone as brightly as the stars (granted, the stars never carried that maniacal gleam).

"Why, I'm as giddy as a schoolgirl," she said. "To *think* that I may finally, *actually* see the inside of the Humphrey home!"

"One to check off on the ol' bucket list."

We climbed the wide cement steps, Mother singing "Master of the House," Sushi whining her objection. I hated that song, too (we were a divided family on the subject of *Les Miz*).

Mother approached the imposing door, studied it like Scrooge seeing Marley's face on the knocker, then, extending her arm straight, rang the bell.

We waited. My mind played the tune *Jeopardy* does when the contestants are writing out their answers.

She rang again.

And again we waited. Dum, dum, dum, dum, dum, dum *dum* . . . or was that *dumb*?

"Not home," I said.

"Nonsense. I saw a curtain ruffle out of the corner of my eye."

Even with glaucoma, the corners of her eyes were twenty-twenty.

The next *ding-dong* brought results, Lyle apparently having reached the conclusion—as had so many Serenity residents before him—that Vivian Borne was not going away.

"Vivian," he acknowledged with a bland little smile, then politely nodded to me. He clearly didn't know my name, despite our various auction encounters.

The childlike chubby man wore a navy silk smoking jacket over a white shirt with no tie, dark slacks, and slippers, looking like a boy playing dress-up in his father's clothes. Assuming there were still fathers around who wore silk smoking jackets.

"Merry Christmas, Lyle," Mother said cheerfully, extending the plate of cookies. "My daughter, Brandy, and I were just thinking about our various friends, as one tends to do at this time of year, and remembered that on our last meeting—at that Wilton auction—we *may* have come off a trifle . . . brusque."

"You called me a horrible little man, Vivian."

"And I am here to apologize and wish you the most felicitous greetings of the season. Please accept these delicious Christmas cookies by way of my amends. . . . May we come in, dear?"

Before he could answer, she thrust the plate of covered cookies into his hands, distracting him as she brazenly pushed by. I followed, giving our very reluctant host my sweetest, most sincere smile. Because, you know, once you learn how to fake sincerity, you've got it made.

Lyle hurried to catch up, as Mother was moving through the large entry hall, with its impressive crystal chandelier and massive antique grandfather clock, on her way to who-knew-where. And wherever that was, I was following right behind, with Sushi under my coat, her head popping out like a cute version of an *Alien* chest-burster.

Our unhappy host blurted, "Ladies! Let's use the parlor, please."

Mother turned and made a sweeping bow. I swear she did.

"Why," she said, "that's very gracious of you, Lyle. I'd love to see the festive treasures I've heard so much about. Your Christmas collection is legendary!"

With a weak smile, put-upon Lyle pushed apart two large, sliding oak doors, and we entered into a twinkling, glittering Christmas cornucopia of eras-gone-by.

Mother and I stood agape.

In the bay window stood an enormous *real* fir tree (thankfully, not upside down), resplendent with antique glass ornaments, tinsel, and large, old-fashioned lights, circa the 1950s. Seated on a Victorian needlepoint couch was a row of bears, several of which I recognized as from Steiff, the venerable German toy company—worth a small furry fortune.

Elsewhere—in this corner, on that table—were other displays of Christmas collectibles: antique Nativity scenes; little candle figures of choir children, Christmas trees, and reindeer; plaster Santa banks, including the one he had outbid Mother over; children's sleds, red wagons, and skates; and an assortment of old parlor games, in their original boxes.

Mother turned to Lyle with eyes so wide behind the magnifying lenses that you'd bet she could spot a flea on a reindeer's derriere.

"My *dear*," she breathed, "never have I seen such an impressive Christmas collection in all my born days . . . and that's *Vivian* Borne days!" She laughed gaily.

Suddenly, our host's demeanor changed. "Why, thank you," he said, beaming back at her. The way to a collector's heart is through his possessions.

I nodded, the room sparkling around me red, white, and green. "It's . . . I mean, it's absolutely breathtaking."

He beamed at me, too. "Thank you. . . . Uh, is that a dog?"

"Yes, I'm sorry . . . I should have left her in the car."

Vivian said, gesturing toward us, "Not to worry. She's housebroken."

I trust she meant Sushi.

"Do . . . do you mind if we sit down?" She raised the back of a hand to her forehead. "This overwhelming array has simply bowled me over. I actually feel a little faint . . ."

Okay, now *that* was faking.

Lyle, concerned, said, "Shall I get you some water, Vivian?"

"No . . . no. I'll be fine." Then she added, "Well, perhaps some eggnog, if you have any handy."

"I do. I'll get it." He handed her back the plate of cookies.

"No rum, though. We're on medication."

"All right, Vivian."

He scurried off.

I asked, "What are you up to?"

She moved over to the edge of an Oriental rug on which was assembled an assortment of old painted cast-iron doorstops; about six to nine inches tall, they included a Christmas tree, reindeer, sleigh, and a bag with presents.

Bending down, risking her knees, her behind high, she glanced back and asked, "Didn't you notice the doorstops?"

"Oh yes." And my next comment reflected information I had that I haven't shared with you yet; if you want fair play, go to bingo at your local church. "Is it there?"

Mother shook her head, and stood abruptly. "Shhh . . . he's coming back." Then, "Follow my lead."

Those three words coming from Mother never failed to chill me to the bone.

Since Sushi was squirming in my arms, I looked for a place to sit down unoccupied by bears, then selected a straight-back Hitchcock next to the tree. I slipped out of my coat, letting it huddle around my shoulders, and settled the pooch on my lap.

Lyle, having returned with a silver tray holding three tumblers of creamy liquid, smiled. "I thought we all might as well have something to drink with the cookies."

Setting the tray gently on the edge of a collectibles-arrayed table, he moved a gaggle of Christmas geese off a settee, and he and Mother sat there.

Mother, fully recovered from her fake fainting spell, removed the plastic wrap from the cookies, and offered him one.

Lyle selected a tree-shaped cookie, took a bite, and closed his eyes. "Say, these are wonderful."

Now it was Mother who beamed. "Thank you."

I guessed if I wanted something, I'd have to get it myself. Even if I *had* been the one to actually bake and frost the cookies.

Mother patted Lyle's knee. "Now, dear—about why we're here. Why we're *really* here, I mean."

Lyle, who had finished one cookie and was on to the next, was nodding. "Bernie Watkins," he managed with his mouth full.

Mother appeared surprised. "Quite right. You *have* heard then? About the terrible tragedy?"

Nodding again, he swallowed. "I heard about it on the radio. And I've spoken to that Bo-Bo individual several times today."

"Really?"

Lyle brushed crumbs from his lap. "Most recently, this afternoon. He called to say that my offer for his stepfather's Christmas collectibles wasn't high enough. That I had competition."

"Do tell!"

"Don't play possum, Vivian. He said your daughter came around and offered to top my prices."

"Well, your quotes were rather . . . what is that crude term? Lowball."

Lyle shrugged, then sipped his eggnog. "I didn't care for his manner. So I told him I was no longer interested."

Mother frowned. "Why is that?"

"Earlier this afternoon, I spoke to Sheriff

Rudder, who knew that I'd done some business with Bernie . . . and I came to understand that my late friend had most likely been murdered." He shivered.

"And this was enough to put you off on the collectibles his stepson was offering?"

"That's right. I told that dreadful Bo-Bo character that I didn't want *anything* to do with 'blood antiques.' "

Mother nodded. "Always dangerous, dealing in ill-begotten gains."

"And you know what he said to that?" Lyle asked aghast. " 'Only the *sleigh* has any blood on it.' "

Mother tsk-tsked, then said, "I most certainly understand, dear boy. But, be that as it may, I thought you might *still* have an interest in Bernie's Coca-Cola Santa doorstop."

Lyle stiffened, his eyes narrowed. "Why would you think that?"

"Well, firstly," she answered matter-of-factly, "it's an extremely rare collectible that Coca-Cola commissioned Haddon Sundblom—the creator of their Coke-swilling Santa—to design in 1931, only for distributors . . . and precious few examples survived the scrap metal drive during the Second World War."

Lyle shifted nervously beside her.

"And secondly," Mother continued, "while the doorstop *is* on the inventory list you compiled for Mr. Ekhardt last Wednesday it's *missing* from the one you gave to Tanya and Bo-Bo . . . today."

That's what I withheld from you. Sorry.

Lyle shrugged. "I typed that list up from the other one, and must have accidentally left the doorstop off. A simple oversight."

From across the room, I put in, "You updated the list, didn't you? To reflect the missing Santa that you'd already taken. Which Bo-Bo and Tanya didn't even know existed."

Lyle stood slowly, looking down at Mother, his nostrils quivering with indignation. "I don't think I care for what you and your daughter are implying."

Mother shrugged. "We're not implying it, Mr. Humphrey. We are *stating* it. You stole that Santa, and we believe you killed to get it."

"Ridiculous! I'm no killer."

Not unkindly, Mother said, "It was likely something of an accident. You sneaked into Bernie's collectibles warehouse, selected that one key item, got caught in the act, and—why, I bet you just reflexively struck out a blow at Bernie with the iron Santa. That doorstop, it wouldn't be the murder weapon by any chance?"

I said, "The police have their own collection of valuable items it can go into."

Lyle smirked, though he was clearly unnerved. "You two have vivid imaginations, but perhaps that's just the, uh, *medication* talking." He pointed toward the door. "I'm afraid you ladies made a trip here for nothing."

Mother said, "Let's give Sheriff Rudder a call and see if he agrees, shall we?"

Grinning yet flustered, Lyle gestured toward his doorstop collection. "Do you *see* the Sundblom Santa?"

Mother sighed. "You'd hardly display it till the smoke had cleared, as they say . . . but I'm sure it's here somewhere."

Lyle's mouth smiled but his eyes didn't. "Perhaps you'd like to have a look around?"

"Oh," Mother said, clapping, "I would simply *love* to see the upstairs!"

She wouldn't want any half-filled buckets on her bucket list, after all.

Lyle leaned forward and his upper lip curled in a sneer. "Well, you *can't*. Get *out*!"

We'd been thrown out of fancier places. Not much fancier, though.

"Lyle," Mother said gently, still not rising, "I know you must have given Bernie a generous offer for the Sundblom piece. You lowballed those dreadful stepchildren, but Bernie knew his onions, and you would have respected his opinion."

His chin crinkled. "I admit that I did try to buy that Santa. I offered twice as much as any had ever gone for. But he had his own plans."

I said, "Yeah, a museum, where everybody could enjoy it. You may love Christmas *stuff*, Mr. Humphrey, but you don't get *Christmas* at all."

"I don't care what you think of me," Lyle said. "But I'm *no* killer."

I set Sushi down on the floor, and was putting on my coat, when Lyle shouted, "What is that creature *doing*? *Stop* that thing!"

At first I thought he meant Mother, that she had tried to make a break for the upstairs maybe; but Lyle was pointing at the "creature" stirring under his tree: Sushi, who was sniffing at a present under there.

And before I could reach the little mutt, those tiny sharp claws had torn away the Christmas wrapping to reveal the cutest Santa doorstop you ever saw.

Chapter Six

And to All a Good Night

Vivian speaking once again.

If this were one of our very entertaining and humorous novels (visit www.BarbaraAllan.com for a complete list), I would enthrall you, dear reader, with Lyle's heartbreaking confession. Why, the man broke down as splendidly as a killer in a courtroom scene on a *Perry Mason* episode!

Of course, including that would be redundant, as I had deduced what occurred—indeed, Lyle, unable to buy the rare doorstop from Bernie, went to the elderly man's place at night, broke into the outbuilding to steal it, and was caught in the act by the owner, whom he clobbered with the cast-iron antique before hiding the body in the sleigh.

But perhaps the lion's (or shih tzu's) share of the credit must go to Sushi, who had sniffed Bernie's blood at the crime scene and sensed its scent under Lyle's Christmas tree, drawing her to the wrapped Santa.

Tanya and Bo-Bo moved into Bernie's house, and I've heard on good authority (the Romeos) that Bo-Bo—handy with a hammer—is making some much-needed repairs.

The most valuable of the Christmas collectibles and the antiques were sold at auction, where they went handsomely well; but I understand that Tanya has held onto enough of them to light up the lawn next year.

Perhaps—to the delight of Serenity's kids of all ages—cars will once again be clogging River Road at Christmastime.

Our apologies, Mr. Fusselman!

A Trash 'n' Treasures Tip

Disturbing the natural patina of antique cast iron will decrease its value; never clean or repaint it. (However, blood can be wiped off with a soft cloth dipped in mineral spirits.)

Antiques Fruitcake

Brandy's quote:

Revenge is a dish best served before it goes off.

—Brandy Borne

Mother's quote:

If you prick us, do we not bleed? . . .
If you poison us, do we not die?

—*The Merchant of Venice*
Act Three, Scene One

SERENITY PLAYHOUSE

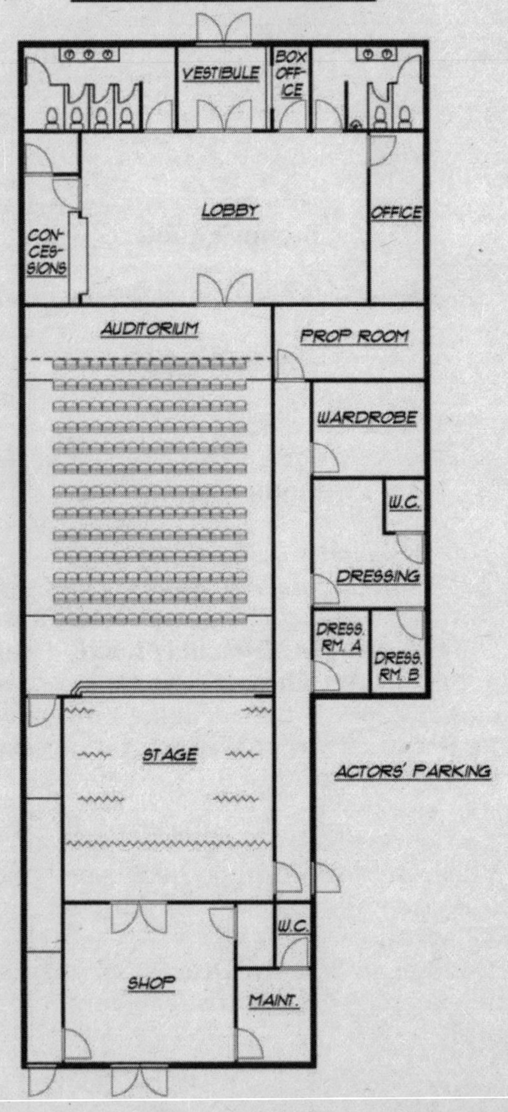

Act One

Have Yourself a Merry Little Fruitcake

Christmas had come to Serenity, Iowa, the downtown windows decorated, lampposts wrapped in evergreen, shoppers laden with packages, snow dusting the sidewalks. Everyone in the land, or at least our little river town, was having a holly jolly holiday season . . . except me. Brandy Borne.

I was miserable.

Why? Because Mother had roped me into helping her with the annual Christmas play at the Playhouse.

(**Mother to Brandy**: Dear, your opening is a little cheerless for a Christmas story, don't you think?)

(**Brandy to Mother**: It's a Christmas story with a murder in it. What do you expect?)

(**Mother to Brandy**: What *I* expect isn't the issue. And, yes, the *readers* expect some mischief and mayhem. But what they *don't* expect is you throwing yourself a pity-party instead of a Christmas one. Are you current on your Prozac, dear?)

(**Brandy to Mother**: Are you current on your lithium?)

(**Editor to Vivian and Brandy**: Ladies, are we going to have an issue again with these asides?)

(**Brandy to Editor**: She started it.)

(**Vivian to Editor:** I think the asides add flavor! And character!)

(**Editor to Vivian and Brandy**: I think it's annoying. And any further extracurricular squabbling between you two will be deleted from the text. But I must agree with Vivian. Brandy, please rewrite the opening.)

Christmas had come to quaint Serenity, nestled along and above the banks of the mighty Mississippi like the star atop a tannenbaum. Ye olde Victorian shop windows were festively decorated, lampposts wrapped in evergreen, twinkling lights strung hither and yon, cheerful shoppers laden with colorful packages frolicking down snow-dusted sidewalks . . . and me?

Why, I was as rosy-cheeked as Old Saint Nick, feeling positively joyous. After all, Mother had been kind enough to allow me to help her put on the annual Christmas play at the Playhouse.

Better?

But before we go merrily Christmas-ing into our murder mystery, let's introduce our cast, or anyway, the two leads. Brandy Borne (me), thirty-two, divorced, bottle-blonde, blue-eyed, and Prozac-popping since coming back to live with her mother. Think Kristen Bell. Mother (her), Vivian Borne, seventies, bipolar, widowed, Danish stock, local thespian, and amateur sleuth. Think Meryl Streep (if Mother herself isn't available).

Of course, actors are cattle, as Hitchcock said. It's the play that's the thing, and the thing in this case was *The Fruitcake That Saved Christmas.*

The play (written by Mother) is based on a true slice of Serenity history dating to the early 1930s during the worst winter of the Great Depression. Most local men had been thrown out of work as business after businesses went bust. One firm that did manage to keep head at least temporarily above water was the Serenity Fruitcake Factory. It, too, seemed about to go down for the third time, when a Christmas miracle occurred.

Franklin Delano Roosevelt, newly elected but not yet in office, took a whistle-stop tour across the country in early December to calm a jittery nation—a tour that included a brief no-speech stop at the train station at the riverfront in Serenity. The president-elect was standing at the railing of the caboose, waving to the crowd of well-wishers, when the owner of the fruitcake factory, Mrs. Hattie Ann Babcock, took the opportunity to rush forward and present him with one of her signature fruitcakes. Roosevelt sampled the cake on the spot and declared it to be the best he'd ever tasted—"Simple with integrity!"—and promptly ordered several hundred as holiday gifts for cronies and constituents.

After the story in the *Serenity Journal* was picked up by the Associated Press, thousands of orders began pouring in from all across the country. Soon the factory began churning out fruitcakes day and night, the expanded shifts putting darn near every able-bodied man in Serenity back to work just in time for Christmas.

Mother—not just the playwright but the director—insisted on using the original factory recipe for her play, and went to some trouble getting it. After all, the Serenity Fruitcake Factory had devolved into a bakery in the 1940s and by the '60s was just a fondly remembered wisp of our community's collective memory.

But after locating a descendant of Mrs. Babcock's on an Internet ancestry site, Mother hounded the poor elderly man by phone till he finally coughed the recipe up. Coughing it up is, coincidentally, what I want to do every time I have a bite of *any* fruitcake.

Thursday morning, for the evening's dress rehearsal, Mother baked two prop fruitcakes: one for Hattie Ann Babcock (Act One), and the other for President Roosevelt (Act Two). Ever thoughtful, Mother wanted fresh fruitcakes for the actors who'd be sampling them onstage.

After supper, Mother—looking take-charge in her navy wool Breckenridge slacks and jacket—and I—loaded for bear in DKNY jeans and Juicy Couture black sweater—gathered our things to leave for the eight o'clock rehearsal at the Playhouse. My brown-and-white diabetic shih tzu, Sushi, could read all the signs and did her take-me-along dance.

The little darling had been blind for several years but now she could see again, thanks to a recent operation. I'd been taking her with me from the first read-through— she just loved being around all that excitement. But as tonight was dress rehearsal, I figured she might get underfoot.

As we bundled up to brave the cold, Sushi spied the fruitcakes in my arms, where by all rights *she* should be, and threw a hissy fit, barking, growling, circling Mother and me like a tree she was considering.

Sushi *had* been neglected most of the day, what with me working at our antiques shop downtown, and Mother preoccupied with last-minute rehearsal details. So I passed the fruitcakes to Mother and scooped Soosh up—it was either that or suffer consequences that could be as minor as coming home to entryway piddle or as major as chewed-up Jimmy Choos.

It was already dark when we piled into the car with me behind the wheel, Mother riding shotgun with Sushi on her lap. I'd put the fruitcakes in the trunk, to keep them away from Sushi, who had a serious jones for those particular baked goods.

You see, when Mother first got hold of that fabled recipe, she tried it out, leaving a fruitcake to cool in its pan on the kitchen counter. The newly sighted Sushi apparently scaled our little red step stool to get up there and help herself. This I deduced, amateur sleuth that I am, from an empty cake pan on the counter and a belly-swollen shih tzu on her back in the middle of the kitchen floor.

So it's safe to say the fruitcake got the Sushi Seal of Approval.

On the ten-mile drive past the city limits to the Playhouse, Mother seemed understandably jittery.

"I hope there's no trouble tonight with the second act," she lamented.

Vivian Borne was still quite attractive at her undisclosed age—porcelain complexion, large blue eyes made bigger by thick glasses, straight nose, wide mouth, wavy silver hair pulled loosely back.

During last night's tech rehearsal, the authentic-looking wood-and-cloth caboose carrying Roosevelt rolled off its tracks, knocking down various bits of scenery.

"I'm hostage to my penchant for realism!" Mother cried. Sushi, in her arms, gave her a "huh?" look.

"Everything will be fine," I soothed. "I'm sure Miguel will have organized all the repairs."

Miguel was stage manager at the Playhouse.

"I know he will, dear," she said. "That's not what's troubling me most."

"What *is*?"

"I just don't know how much more I can *abide* from that woman! The one thing I cannot *tolerate* in theater is a *diva*!"

Pot, meet kettle. Kettle, meet pot.

Mother was referring to her leading lady, Madeline de Morlaye, who had, since the beginning of rehearsals, been a real pain where the sun does not shine. Mother had known de Morlaye for decades, going back to when the woman's real name was a decidedly untheatrical Hildegard Gooch.

Madeline, somewhere in a plastic-surgery no-woman's land between fifty and sixty, had grown up in Serenity, but left about thirty years ago to find her fame and fortune on the Great White Way. She'd had some success mostly off- but occasionally on Broadway, and had been in bus-and-truck productions as recently as a few years ago.

Though still quite attractive, Madeline's beauty had faded enough (Mother cattily opined) to keep her off the stage and the casting couches that had helped put her there. And now she had found her way back to Serenity, where she was still a local-girl-made-good legend.

Or was that Gooch-made-good?

What really irked Mother was that she herself had lobbied to play the part of Hattie Ann Babcock. But the Playhouse board of directors gently if firmly ruled that since Mother was the playwright *and* director, she had enough on her plate. After all, she was reminded, the Playhouse doesn't present one-woman shows.

Or anyway they hadn't since Mother starred in and wrote *Give 'Em Heck, Eleanor!* (Lots of Republicans had demanded their money back.)

Privately (and this got back to Mother), the board felt Madeline would be the bigger draw because she had performed on Broadway and, therefore, was a "legitimate" actress. Plus, Madeline was younger. A slap on both Mother's cheeks. You decide what cheeks.

Right now Mother was saying disdainfully, "I wrote a serious play and *she's* turning it into a *melodrama*!"

I restrained myself from pointing out that Mother had written the Depression-era banker character as a Snidely Whiplash-type right down to curling mustache, black cape and top hat.

"I'll *tell* you why she's a diva!" Mother blurted.

This was a response to a question I hadn't asked.

She was spitting words out as if they tasted foul: "Insisting on a private dressing room . . . Baccara bottled water . . . fresh fruit . . . personal masseuse. . . ."

No wonder Mother was mad; her past theatrical perks had never included a masseuse. She did demand M&Ms, but was never fussy about what color.

Thankfully, my turn off the main highway lay just ahead in another moment I was driving down the long, snowy lane to the Playhouse, passing by cornfields on either side, where currently the only crop was snow.

The theater began as an old barn where community actors would gather and perform on a makeshift stage to the delight of family and friends. You could almost hear Judy Garland and Mickey Rooney yelling, "Come on, gang—let's put on a show and save the farm!"

Over the years, the barn had been transformed

into a modern theatrical facility, with new additions, and a state-of-the art auditorium. About the only thing left of the original structure was its rooster weather vane.

Mother had been a big part of this transformation, as any play Vivian Borne appeared in (or directed) always drew crowds because *anything could happen.* Like the time she was playing the lead in a musical version of *Everybody Loves Opal,* while enthusiastically mugging for the audience, and stepped off the apron into the orchestra pit and got her right foot stuck in the tuba. Or when she was directing *My Fair Lady* and had several real horses run across the stage in the Ascot scene, causing a panic in the auditorium, not to mention some messy cleanup.

I parked the car among others in the lot reserved for players and staff and we got out, Mother carrying Sushi, while I liberated the two fruitcakes from the trunk and carted them in.

No sooner had we entered the stage door than Miguel rushed up to Mother, frantic. He was quickly joined by Paul, the lighting designer, and Martha, our wardrobe supervisor.

"We've got a problem," Miguel said. About thirty, with dark wavy hair and an athletic body, he had joined the Playhouse as an assistant stage manager, but his organizational skills and ability to oversee all departments soon led to the removal of "assistant."

"*Two* problems," added Paul. Slender, bearded, about forty, Paul had a long tenure with the Playhouse, during which he won several regional awards for exceptional and innovative lighting.

"Make that three," said Martha. The big-boned woman in her midfifties sported mannishly cut gray hair. She'd joined the Playhouse this past season, after taking early retirement from teaching drama at the community college.

Mother sighed and set down Sushi, who trotted off per usual to find Kimberly, Madeline's understudy, who was inclined to spoil Soosh with doggie treats.

Mother asked, "These problems wouldn't, by any chance, have anything to do with our distinguished leading lady?"

"*Yes,*" the trio answered.

"Very well . . . a director's job is to solve problems. Let's take them one at a time. Paul?"

He gestured in frustration. "She's demanding that I change the lighting, to her specs—says what I've come up with is unflattering. I told her that that's *impossible* at this late stage, but she said . . . Well, I can't repeat it in mixed company. In *any* company!"

Mother turned her gaze to Martha. "And you, my dear?"

The wardrobe woman grunted. "Our star refuses to wear a certain costume."

"Which one would that be?"

"The fruitcake factory uniform. She says it's too drab. She says the owner of the firm wouldn't wear a uniform."

Mother nodded. "That's two." She looked at Miguel. "Hit me with number three."

He sighed. "There isn't exactly a number three. It's just that I *should,* as stage manager, be able to solve Paul and Martha's problems without bothering *you*. But Madeline won't listen to me!"

Mother smiled benevolently. "Not to worry, dears. I'll speak with our darling diva. May I assume she is in her dressing room?"

"You may," Miguel said with a smirk. Then added, under his breath, "The witch."

Or anyway something that rhymed with "witch."

Mother clapped her hands. "All right, now, children! Back to work! Tarry not! We have a dress rehearsal to put on."

And the trio left, but I wouldn't call it not tarrying.

"Well, good luck with your star talent," I said. "Untalented little me is off to the prop room."

Mother stopped me with a traffic cop's upraised palm. "No, dear, I want you to accompany me."

"What for?"

"Moral support."

"What kind of moral support?"

"The kind where you help me refrain from strangling that woman."

We headed down the hallway to the dressing area, which was divided into two large rooms—one for the actresses, the other for actors, with private quarters for the two leads. We stopped at a door with a placard that should have read, MADELINE DE MORLAYE, but someone had switched the removable letters around so that it said, MADELINE DE MORE LAY.

Mother regarded this revision with a raised eyebrow. "Tasteless. Tactless. True."

Then she knocked once.

"Go . . . ay . . . *way*!"

"Interesting line reading," Mother said to me, and went in.

Madeline, in a white robe, was seated at her cosmetic table, her back to us. Stage makeup on, she wore a short black finger-waved wig.

"Oh, it's *you,*" Madeline said, addressing Mother's reflection in the mirror with open contempt. "I thought it was that horrible fat girl again. Always knocking, telling me how much time I have until curtain."

How thoughtless of her.

While Mother walked deeper into the lioness's den, I remained in the doorway, out of range of flying brushes and cosmetic bottles.

"Dear," Mother began, "I hear you're unhappy with the lighting."

The actress whirled around in her chair. "And for good reason! I happened to see some camera footage one of the minor cast members took from the audience, and that ghastly lighting makes me look ten years older!"

Older than what? To validate her claim, one would have to establish what her *real* age was.

"Madeline," Mother said, her voice more soothing and low-key than she ever used in talking to me, "surely a trained professional, like yourself, is aware that any concerns you may have had with the lighting scheme should have been addressed at tech rehearsal. We're past the point of no return on that front."

Madeline opened wide her red-painted mouth to object, but Mother raised a conciliatory finger. "*But* . . . perhaps Paul can make a few adjustments.

I'll advise the use of flattering filters. Will that be all right?"

"I suppose," the actress replied sourly.

"Now," Mother continued, pulling up a chair, getting chummy, "regarding your costume in Act One, which you deem to be drab. This is the Depression, dear, and the factory is failing. The real Hattie Ann wore the uniform as a show of solidarity with her workers. Knowing your dedication to realism, I can't imagine you'd wear anything else."

Again, Madeline began to protest, again, Mother brought forth the finger.

"*But,*" Mother went on, "perhaps Martha has time before opening night to make some figure-flattering alterations. Remember, dear, Marilyn Monroe looked stunning in a potato sack!"

Madeline sighed, weight of the world. "Fine, fine, *fine* . . . I'll wear the dismal thing."

"Very good, dear. Now, is there anything else I can do for you?"

"Yes," Madeline snapped. "You can find out who put a *dead rat* in my dressing room!"

A dead rat? Put in her dressing room? Why didn't I think of that!

Madeline was saying, "Such a sick, cruel joke to play!"

Mother frowned but her eyes were wide. "Where is it?"

"Well, it's not here *now*! I had that clod of a janitor remove it."

She meant Leroy, the maintenance man.

Since Mother didn't seem to have a placating

answer for her in the dead-rat department, I said, "I doubt anybody put a dead rat in here, Miss de Morlaye."

Madeline glanced at me as if noticing my presence for the first time; maybe she was. "Oh?"

I nodded. "Leroy says there's been a recent infestation at the Playhouse. I guess they're coming in from the cornfields to get warm."

"Well," Madeline huffed, "it had better not happen again."

Mother's smile was strained. "Yes, of course. I'll see that it doesn't."

I said, helpfully, "Leroy says he's put traps out."

Madeline turned back to her mirror. We were dismissed without a good-bye. Not that I cared.

And we left, closing the door.

In the hall, Mother whispered, "Actors! They're such *children*."

She was telling me? I had witnessed plenty of Mother's own theatrical tirades; but in her defense, she was better on her worst day than Madeline on her best.

I said, "*Now* can I go to the prop room? Unless you have other battles to fight that require my moral support."

"Not at the moment, dear. I'll let you know. But thank you."

She gave me a corny half bow, and we separated.

How I loved the prop room! Where else could you find a shrunken head, a Roman helmet, a gorilla suit, fake snowballs, or a gun that fired flowers, all under one roof? And where else in a busy theater, bustling with the needs of a soon-to-be-presented production, could you hide away and maybe even take a nap?

Not that I was doing much napping on the job. I was in charge of hand props, which is to say any item (not part of a costume) that an actor needs when making his or her entrance.

Like the two fruitcakes.

One cake (used in the factory scene, where Hattie Ann taste-tests her product) I placed on a serving plate; the other one (presented to President Roosevelt at the train depot) I wrapped in a white linen cloth. Then I gathered the few other necessary props, put everything in a box, and left. No napping tonight.

On my way back to the stage area, I passed Madeline's dressing room, where Clara, the assistant stage manager, was about to knock on the door.

Clara was a high-school student earning extra credit for her drama class; quiet, pleasant, she mostly swept up and fetched things, and called curtain time for the actors.

"Fifteen minutes, Miss de Morlaye," the pudgy, plain girl called out.

To which, Madeline yelled, "I've got a *clock,* you imbecile!"

The first time Madeline abused her verbally, I thought Clara might cry. She'd told me during backstage downtime how much she admired the actress.

This time, the girl didn't flinch.

Just the same, I said, "She's been a witch to everybody tonight. I know Mother's talked to her about it. Sorry it didn't do any good."

"Oh, it did some good."

"Yeah?"

She nodded and smiled. "She used to call me a '*fat* imbecile.' " Then she started off, looking over her shoulder. "If you see Miguel, would you tell him I'm helping Martha in wardrobe?"

"Sure."

Backstage, I found Sushi with Kimberly, Madeline's understudy, who also had a small part in the first act as a factory cook; she was very talented, and if Madeline walked off in a snit, Kimberly would be ready to step into the role.

Pretty, in her midtwenties, with long blond hair the color of corn tassels, Kimberly perched on a stool inside the wings, stage right. She made the drab factory costume look just fine. On her lap was a very contented Sushi, who practically purred as Kimberly stroked her fur.

I couldn't help but feel a pang of jealousy.

Oh, sure, I knew Soosh loved me, and I was her master, but like all canines, the fickle little mutt's affections could be bought with a single doggie treat.

"Hi, Brandy," Kimberly said with a smile, then looked down at Sushi. "Such an angel."

Such a devil.

I placed my box on a nearby table used for props, then laid them out in the order in which they were needed. My duties completed, I took another stool next to Kimberly, and Sushi jumped over to me, perhaps sensing my jealousy, or remembering who filled her dog dish daily.

"Our star's really on the rampage tonight," I said.

"So I hear," Kimberly replied, shaking her head. "Miguel said she was causing trouble with Paul and Martha."

Miguel and the pretty understudy had become an item. Mother once asked me why I preferred to remain backstage and not watch from out front, and I told her that's where the *real* drama is.

Kimberly and I sat quietly after that, the hustle and bustle right before curtain making it tough to converse any further, including the orchestra in the pit beginning to tune.

Even though Mother's play was not a musical per se, she had insisted on five-piece accompaniment—piano, trumpet, clarinet, sax and drum—that would perform Depression music during the overture, scene transitions, intermission, and finale. They did well by "Brother, Can You Spare a Dime," "Pennies from Heaven," and "Stormy Weather," along with more upbeat numbers like "Happy Days Are Here Again" and "We're in the Money."

Sushi, hearing the musical instruments, jumped down from my lap and trotted off through the wing and down the small flight of stairs from the stage to the auditorium, where she would watch from her usual place—row five, middle section, seat ten—perched on a pillow provided by Mother.

Having attended every rehearsal, Sushi had

become so familiar with the play she seemed to know every actor's entrance and exit. One time, when the actor playing the mayor missed his cue because he was outside the stage door having a smoke, Sushi barked, as if to say, "Hey, where the hell *are* you, bud?"

Tonight I wanted to see the play as the audience would, and after Madeline appeared for her stage-right entrance, I abandoned my stool and went out into the auditorium, settling into a seat toward the back, for a better perspective.

Except for Mother, myself, and Sushi, the only other person in the audience was Martha, on hand in case Madeline threw another s—t fit about her costume.

The overhead lights dimmed, the orchestra began the overture, and it was magic time!

ACT ONE, SCENE ONE:

(*As the final notes from the orchestra fade away, the curtain rises slowly on a dreary factory room, where a conveyor belt carries fruitcakes along, a half-dozen male factory workers in gray overalls guiding their progress, this one applying candied cherries, that one nuts, another powdered sugar, etc.)*

(**Aside from Brandy:** Originally, I ran the conveyor belt, but kept making it go so fast that fruitcakes fell off, like in that *I Love Lucy* episode . . . so Leroy took over.)

Hattie Anne Babcock/Madeline: (enters stage right, pauses for audience applause before addressing the workers)
Everyone, please gather around! I have an important announcement to make.

(The workers leave their posts and form a semicircle around Hattie.)

Hattie: (shakes head, sighs)

I hate to tell you this, my loyal workers, my friends . . . but I'm afraid I'm going to have to close the factory.

(Groans and murmurs from the workers.)

Hattie: (frustrated)

Due to the depression, the cost of candied fruits and nuts has gone sky-high. And Prohibition has effectively put an end to adding rum to our cakes. I can see no other option than shutting down production.

(more groans and murmurs)

One male worker: (stepping forward)

Ma'am, why can't we get certain ingredients from the black market? I know a fellow who—

Hattie: (emphatically)

No! Absolutely not. I won't do business with speakeasy ruffians! That's not the American way!

Female cook/Kimberly: (offstage)

Oh, Mrs. Babcock! Mrs. Babcock!

(Hattie turns toward voice.)

Female cook: (entering; holding plate with fruitcake)

Mrs. Babcock, do you remember the original factory recipe? Before we jazzed it up, I mean?

Hattie: (a bit cross)

Yes, of course I do. It was a simple recipe, but delicious and had integrity. What does that have to do with our predicament?

Female cook: (with excitement)

Well, why don't we go back to producing *that* fruitcake?

(hopeful murmurs from the workers)

Suddenly Madeline broke character, walked downstage to the orchestra pit, peered out into the darkness, located Mother, and shouted, "I've raised this with you before, Vivian, and nothing was done about it! Is this scene about *me*, or the stupid *cook*?"

My mouth dropped open. Never had I witnessed an actor interrupt a final run-through at the Playhouse. It was a theatrical no-no anywhere.

Mother leapt from her seat like a jack-in-the-box. "Madame! This is dress rehearsal! Return to your position!"

Madeline stood her ground, glowering, and for a moment, I thought she might walk out. But then, with a grimace and a sigh that was half-growl, she retraced her steps.

Mother cried, *"Resume!"*

Hattie: (addressing cook)

I'm going to want to test the old recipe first. Would you make one?

Female cook: (thrusting plate forward)

Why, I already have. This is the original fruitcake. I took the liberty of making a sample.

Hattie: (taking fruitcake)

Oh, you clever girl. Let me test the cake to see if it's as good as I remember. . . .

(Hattie takes plate, breaks off piece of fruitcake, eats it.)

Again, Madeline broke character, this time by spitting the fruitcake on the floor.

"You expect me to eat *that*!" she shouted toward Mother. "My lord, woman! It's *rancid*!"

Mother, exasperated, said, "Must you exaggerate, my dear? Move along!"

The actress grabbed at her chest.

For a second it seemed like overacting, more of the melodrama Mother had complained about from her leading lady. But then Madeline's body went into convulsions, and she dropped to her knees, fell over on one side, and rolled over on her back.

The convulsions ceased.

Madeline lay still.

As the actors stood stunned, frozen in place, a hush falling over the theater, Mother rushed up onto the stage. I was not far behind her, sprinting down the aisle, Sushi not far behind me.

Someone said, "My God. I think she's had a heart attack!"

Someone else muttered, "She'd have to *have* a heart."

Mother, kneeling next to Madeline, put two fingers on the woman's throat.

"Mother?" I asked.

But I didn't hold out much hope that the woman was breathing. Our star's face was an ashen mask, open eyes staring up at the stage lights, but not seeing.

Mother stood. Shook her head. "I'm afraid the dying scene we've just witnessed was quite real."

A visibly shaken Kimberly asked, “How can you be sure? We should call the paramedics.”

“Doing so would be a waste of time and taxpayers’ money.” Now it was her turn to be melodramatic: “Madeline was poisoned by the fruitcake.”

Someone asked, “How do you know?”

Mother pointed to Sushi, who had sniffed the fruitcake and backed away, repulsed. “Tell them, dear,” she said to me.

“Because,” I said, “Sushi’s not eating it.”

Act Two

It's Beginning to Look a Lot Like Fruitcake

Dearest ones!

This is Vivian talking/writing. I do apologize for interrupting Brandy's enthralling narrative, but I'm afraid I must clarify and correct a few statements she's made. That child has *quite* the vivid imagination. Where do you suppose she got it? (I would attach a smiley face here, but both Brandy and our editor have forbidden me the use of emoticons. Which is in itself worthy of a frowny face.)

Contrary to what Brandy said/wrote, I did *not* take a tumble into the orchestra pit and get my right foot stuck in a tuba. How big does she think my feet *are*? I got my *left* foot stuck in the bell of a baritone.

Furthermore, I did *not* send horses running across the stage—for heaven's sake, how could they get up to speed? They just trotted across, and there were only two of them. (I couldn't fit any more backstage.)

Brandy *was* correct, however, in saying the horses caused something of a panic in the audience, and poor Mrs. Sneidecker (the mayor's wife) fainted dead away. But His Honor's better half had plenty of time to recover during our impromptu bonus intermission as we (shall we say) did a little tidying up of the stage before proceeding. Where there are apples, there comes the harvest!

All I can say is that someone with such a delicate constitution as Mrs. Sneidecker should not have selected a ringside seat for one of my productions. Definitely *not* my bad.

On with our dramatic presentation.

After determining that Madeline had made her final curtain call, I asked everyone—actors, stagehands, musicians—to take seats in the auditorium, leaving at least two empty seats between filled ones. *And* to refrain from speaking to each another.

As a skilled investigator, I knew that much as a crime scene can be contaminated, so can the stories of witnesses, if they are allowed to intermingle and compare notes. What each may have seen that might be relevant to the murder must be preserved.

I then called Sheriff Rudder on my cell (like our chief of police, he's on speed dial), since the death occurred in his jurisdiction.

But for a few sobs and sniffles, cast and crew took my direction well, waiting in silence. I took note of who appeared upset, and who did not, and began assembling a mental list of suspects—my "top picks" you might say.

Before long my imposed silence was broken by the faint wail of a siren, growing ever louder, and as heads turned in that direction, I dispatched Brandy to wait out in front of the Playhouse to meet the sheriff.

A few minutes later, Sheriff Rudder came striding down the center aisle, a tall, beefy, imposing figure, who—if I were to squint or remove my glasses, anyway—reminded me of the older John Wayne; he even had the Duke's sideways gait. Affectation or bunions? Who could say?

In Rudder's wake, trying to keep up, came a deputy named Jim Something, a scarecrow of a man with a long face and unruly brown hair, who reminded me of nobody. Not even Ray Bolger.

Rudder came to a stop in front of me with a shudder, like an old car. I stood poised with the orchestra pit just behind me.

"Okay, Vivian," he said gruffly. "Where's the body this time?"

That seemed a trifle gratuitous.

"Downstage left," I replied.

He squinted as if trying to bring me into focus. *"Where?"*

Apparently, the Philistine law enforcer knew little of stage lingo.

Brandy, wandering up next to me, interjected, "She's up on the stage, Sheriff."

Rudder ascended the steps (audience left), walked over to Madeline's prone form, and knelt to examine her. After a long thirty seconds, he straightened and came to the edge of the stage.

"Who is she?" he asked looking down at me.

"Madeline de Morlaye," I said.

His eyebrows climbed his forehead. "No kidding? I heard about her all my life, but I don't remember ever actually *seeing* her. Where are the paramedics?"

"I didn't call them. I called *you*."

"Vivian, my God, why didn't you—"

"My dear sheriff, what would they accomplish at this late stage . . . no pun intended . . . other than contaminate the crime scene? Call them yourself, if you think it prudent."

His eyes were wide, eyebrows still high. "You're saying she was murdered?"

Rather slow picking up his cues tonight, our sheriff.

"*Yes,* she was murdered," I said. "Sushi wouldn't eat the fruitcake! Do pay attention."

(In retrospect, I may have skipped a step or two. But I was very upset, having lost a very old and dear friend to person or persons unknown.)

Sheriff Rudder was descending the steps (audience right this time). "By God, I thought you knew better than to joke about things like this, Vivian—"

"She's not, Sheriff," Brandy interjected. "We're sure the fruitcake Madeline ate onstage had been poisoned. Sushi is crazy about the stuff and turned her nose up at the one Madeline ate a bite from. It's a play prop? We were in dress rehearsal?"

Rudder had the look of a man who'd been soundly slapped. He took a few moments to process Brandy's nicely concise summary, then grunted, looked from Brandy to me, decided we were telling the truth, and used his cell to call the coroner and a forensics team.

And the paramedics, I will admit, for transfer of the body to the hospital morgue.

Then the sheriff turned his attention to a captive audience of witnesses more used to being onstage or in back of it than out front.

"All right, everyone," he said, loud enough to be heard at the back of the house (nice projection!). "My deputy will begin taking names and addresses. If anyone has *pertinent* information about what happened, speak up at that time, because I'll be wanting to interview you myself. In the meantime, get comfy—this may take a while."

A female stagehand called out, "Can we use our cell phones? I'd like to notify my babysitter."

"For that kind of purpose, yes." Rudder paused. "I suppose it's too late to ask you people not to text about this?"

When more than a few had shrunk in their seats, he grimaced. He had quite a range of expressions! When this was over, I might invite him to try out for Big Daddy opposite my Big Mama in the musical version of *Cat on a Hot Tin Roof* I was planning. (Though I hadn't ruled out playing Maggie the Cat just yet.)

As Deputy Jim began gathering personal information, I took Rudder to one side. Brandy had taken a seat in the audience with Sushi in her lap, near enough to eavesdrop. Good girl.

"Sheriff," I said confidentially, "I have several strong suspects who might benefit from the ol' third-degree treatment."

"Afraid I left my rubber hose home, Vivian."

"You know what I mean, Sheriff—interrogate them! Or is the current preferred term 'interview'? Not that there's anything politically correct about murder."

Rudder gazed at me like I was a window that needed cleaning. But he asked, "Strong suspects, you say?"

"I do indeed. I know this place inside out and these people like the back of my hand. Or should I say, I know these people inside out, and this place like the back of my hand? Six of one!"

He sighed but he was mulling it. "I *would* like a suspect list from you, Vivian. That might be helpful."

"I am here but to serve." I bowed and rolled my hands as if he were a pasha. Straightening, I added, "Furthermore, might I suggest that we use Madeline's dressing room for the interrogations? That is, interviews?"

"Why's that? Wait a minute, *we*?"

"It could make the killer mighty uncomfortable, don't you think? Especially if I were to spray the room with Madeline's signature perfume. What a ghostly touch!"

"Yes, to using Madeline's dressing room. No, to the perfume bit. And *hell* no, to the 'we.' "

I laid a gentle hand on his brawny shoulder.

"I offer my services only because I happen to know certain intimate details about each of the suspects that might prove helpful in establishing motive."

He was looking at my hand like a butterfly had lit upon his shoulder. Only he didn't seem to like butterflies.

"*Obviously* you would be in charge," I cooed. "I would be but a mouse in the corner, not making a peep unless called on. Of course, mice don't peep, but you catch my drift."

He raised a warning finger. "No interrupting."

I put a hand to my chest. "I wouldn't *dream* of violating your trust, Sheriff. I am but a supporting player in your dramatic inquiry."

He smirked, overplaying a little, I thought. "Yeah. Right."

"And might I also suggest that you, without further ado, seal off the maintenance closet?"

"And why is that?"

"Because, dear sir, it contains a most interesting array of poisons."

While the sheriff went off to do that very thing, I beat a fast track to Madeline's dressing room to search for clues.

I began with the dressing table—a messy array of stage makeup and used cotton balls—then checked the pockets of Madeline's street clothes, along with the contents of her purse, looking for notes or correspondence that might be of interest, but I found nothing helpful. A quick rummage through the wastepaper basket also garnered nothing. But I did take time to use my cell to snap pictures of the murder victim's quarters.

I picked up Madeline's play script, which she'd left on a side table, tore out a page, and on the back, wrote down my list of suspects:

Leroy, janitor
Paul, lighting designer
Martha, wardrobe supervisor
Miguel, stage manager
Kimberly, understudy

Of course, the prime suspects of the poisoned fruitcake included myself and Brandy—cook and caretaker. Those names I admitted, I omit. That is, omitted, I admit.

The sheriff arrived shortly accompanied by a Sushi-carrying Brandy, who'd shown him to the dressing room.

"Ah, Brandy dear," I said to her. "I'm delighted you accompanied our noble sheriff."

She gave me that blank look of hers. (Sushi's was much more expressive.) "You are? Why?"

"Well, first order of business in this inquiry is to clear ourselves."

She nodded. "Good point."

Brandy and I sat on the couch, and I filled in a pacing Rudder about our direct involvement, after which, he said, "While you have means and opportunity, neither of you girls has much of a motive."

"Thank you," I said. At my age being called a "girl" has such a nice ring to it.

"I said *much* of one. I'll still need to get formal statements down from both of you. But that comes *later.*"

"Sheriff," Brandy said, leaning forward. Sushi on her lap seemed to be listening intently. "The fruitcake could *only* have been poisoned between the time I put it on the prop table—around seven forty-five—and when it was carried out onstage at about eight-fifteen."

I said, "We're in a unique position, Sheriff, in that with Brandy backstage, and *moi* in the audience, we have between us the ability to determine who, besides ourselves, had opportunity."

Rudder was nodding.

I beamed at him. "And here is what you've been waiting for, Sheriff," I said, handing him the script page. "My list of suspects."

The sheriff looked it over, then spoke into his shoulder walkie-talkie, "Jim, find this Leroy character—he's the janitor—and bring him back to the star dressing room."

Rudder moved the chair from Madeline's dressing table to the center of the room. Brandy and I remained on the couch with Sushi settled between us.

A few minutes later, the deputy delivered Leroy, then stood waiting for his next instructions, which came by way of the sheriff shooing him away like a pesky skeeter.

"Please sit, Leroy," Rudder said, gesturing to the chair. "May I call you that?"

"It's my name," the janitor said, sitting, slumping. He was a big, strapping individual, decked out in overalls and a plaid shirt and work boots—

pale, balding, but with the ghost of a handsome young man lurking in his late middle-aged features.

"You understand," the sheriff said, seeking no chair for himself, preferring to loom, "that this is just a preliminary interview."

"Do I . . . do I need a lawyer?"

"Do you feel the need to have one present? You're not at this stage a suspect or person of interest, just a witness. And I figured it would be easier for you to answer a few simple questions here and now than a bunch of more complicated ones later on, over at the county jail."

Sly fox, our sheriff. You had to admire him for that.

"No," Leroy said quickly, "no, this is fine."

"Good," Rudder said with a friendly smile. "As the janitor, you're in charge of the maintenance room?"

"Yes."

"What sort of things do you keep in there?"

Leroy shrugged. "Usual this and that—brooms, mops, cleaners."

"Any of the cleaning stuff poisonous?"

Leroy hesitated. "Well, yes. Nothing you'd want a small child to get at or anything."

"Such as?"

"Rat poison comes to mind. We've been having a problem with them lately. Out in the country like this. This used to be a barn, you know."

"Pellet type?"

"Powdered. Mice will eat pellets, but rats are smarter."

"Any other poisons?"

Leroy shifted in the chair. Shrugged. "Arsenic."

"What do you use that for?"

"For when the rat poison doesn't do the job."

Rudder paced for a few moments, then asked, "Is the maintenance room kept locked?"

Leroy shook his head. "Only when I leave for the night. Nothin' worth stealin'."

"So anyone who might be at the Playhouse, cast and crew for example, would have access to that room during the day?"

The janitor nodded.

"Thanks, Leroy. This is all very helpful."

Leroy's dull eyes brightened. "Is that all?"

"Just one more question." The sheriff put some oomph into his next line reading: "Where were *you* between seven forty-five and eight-fifteen tonight?"

The janitor frowned in thought. "Let's see . . . I woulda been backstage to operate the conveyor belt durin' that time and maybe a little before."

"Conveyor belt?"

Brandy put in, "It's part of the play." She briefly explained, adding, "The prop fruitcake was on a little table backstage. I wasn't attending it right then. Actors and crew would pass right by it. Before that, it was in my care."

Rudder nodded, then turned to Leroy. "Which means you had ample opportunity to tamper with the fruitcake."

Leroy looked startled. "Me and how many others! But why would I? I had no reason to kill Madeline."

Just a little mouse on the couch, I peeped, "Oh, but you *did*, Leroy. A very *old* reason."

He swiveled in the chair toward me. "I don't know what you could be referrin' to, Vivian."

I said, "Sheriff, once upon a time, back when Madeline de Morlaye was Hildegard Gooch, and Leroy had all his hair and the reputation of a recent high-school football hero, the two got married. Then, less than a year later, the bride skipped town with their scant savings, leaving behind a mountain of charge card debt."

The janitor stared down at his hands.

The sheriff said, "You care to comment on that, Leroy?"

He raised his chin, his eyes wet and glittering with pain and memory. "It's true enough. She left me in a hell of a fix. Lost my business—I had a trophy shop, 'cause I'd been an athlete and people still respected me back then. I wound up losin' my house . . . had to declare bankruptcy. Worked factory jobs awhile, then lately . . . maintenance."

Rudder nodded. "What sort of reunion did you two have here at the Playhouse?"

"That's what hurt me the most, Sheriff. The way Hildie treated me during this production—like *I* had done *her* wrong. And do you know, at first, she pretended not even to *recognize* me?" He gulped air. "All right, so maybe I did have a reason to want to kill her. But I didn't. *I didn't.* You know why?"

"Why, Leroy?"

"I still love her."

He began to weep, and Brandy got up and

showed him out. Such a good heart, my little girl. But all I felt about Leroy was a sense that he was a very, very good suspect.

Oh, think ill of me if you must! But you have to be tough to be a good detective! Hard-boiled. Merciless. And if Brandy should tell you that I got teary-eyed myself, remind her that such moisture is a side effect of my glaucoma medication.

Next in the chair was Paul. The lighting designer, his anxiety apparent, nonetheless readily agreed to questioning.

To Rudder's inquiry of where he'd been between seven forty-five and eight-fifteen, Paul responded, "No surprises there. I was in the lighting booth in back of the auditorium."

Brandy discreetly shook her head.

Catching that, Rudder asked Paul, "The *entire* time?"

"Ah . . . no," Paul corrected. "I guess, come to think of it, I *did* leave the booth for a short while—about a quarter to eight. Vivian asked me to make an adjustment to the stage lights after Madeline complained about them."

Rudder said, "Would that put you in the vicinity of the prop table?"

He shrugged and grinned nervously. "Well, yes, in order to get to the stage lights scaffolding, I had to walk by it—but so did just about everybody."

"What about the maintenance room?"

"What about it?"

"Did you go near it this evening?"

"No. Why would I?" He frowned, shifted in

the chair. "Look, Sheriff, I had *no* reason to kill Madeline. None at all."

From the couch the little mouse peeped again: "Paul, dear, perhaps it's best you throw some light on your affair with our leading lady . . . however brief it may have been. Back in the early stages of preparing for our production?"

Paul seemed to be deciding whether to scowl or start crying. "How is that any kind of . . . of murder motive? It ended amicably enough."

"I hardly think so," I replied. "After your wife found out about the dalliance, she filed for divorce, didn't she?"

"We'd been having other problems—"

"And you had a problem of your *own,* when Madeline dropped you and set her sights on Miguel. She always was a fickle pickle!"

Paul was shaking his head and there was something almost pleading in his tone and manner now. "Vivian, that affair, and Jenny filing for divorce . . . that was just a speed bump. Maybe you haven't heard, but we're getting back together. But I *am* guilty of one thing."

The sheriff sat forward. "Yes?"

Brandy sat forward. "Yes?"

And I sat forward. "Yes?"

"I purposely gave that monster unflattering lighting." He paused. "Want a *real* motive, Sheriff? Ask *Martha* if Madeline didn't find out that our esteemed wardrobe mistress was selling costumes and pocketing the money."

First I'd heard of this!

Paul was saying, "Madeline read her the Riot Act and threatened to go to the board."

That was a motive! And what *is* the Riot Act, anyway?

Rudder asked, "Paul, what makes you privy to this damning information?"

Another shrug. "Madeline told me. Pillow talk, before I got dumped."

Shortly, when the wardrobe supervisor occupied the suspect chair, mannish Martha snapped, "That's a damn lie!"

She swiveled toward me. "Vivian, I *swear* to you, I've never sold costumes for personal gain. Why would I jeopardize my job at the Playhouse, not to mention my reputation? I *demand* to know who said that!"

Rudder, who had not mentioned Paul, said, "Ah . . . let's just say it's come up."

"If you're going to assault me with scurrilous rumors, Sheriff, I have a mind not to answer any more of your questions!"

Rudder had painted himself into a corner, so I said indignantly, "Sheriff, you must cease besmirching this woman's good name! You need to lay this foul rumor to rest. A check of the inventory list against the costumes in wardrobe should clear this up, toot-sweet."

Then to Martha, I asked sweetly, if not tootly, "What do you think of that solution, dear?"

The woman glared at me.

"Well, Martha?" Rudder asked. "Is that our next step? Check the inventory?"

The wardrobe supervisor sighed unhappily. "All right, okay . . . maybe I *did* sell a few old moth-riddled costumes. But all of what I got went back into the costume account—every penny!"

I asked, "Was that *before* or *after* Madeline threatened to go to the board, dear?"

"Well . . . I guess, uh . . . after. But that was an accident of timing."

"Ah, but timing is everything! Especially in the theater. And murder."

Martha adjusted her weight in the chair. "Whatever. I didn't kill her. I don't mourn her, but I didn't kill her."

Rudder said, "No?"

"No. But I . . . I did put that dead rat in her dressing room. There's no law against that, and didn't *that* feel *good*!"

Bad reviews come in all forms.

Rudder asked Martha about the crucial half hour.

She said, "I was in wardrobe, where else?"

"You didn't leave that room?"

"No."

Brandy interjected, "But I *saw* you backstage."

Martha frowned at her, then said, "Oh. Yeah. Forgot. I did grab a smoke."

I asked, "Where?"

"Out the stage door."

"Which took you backstage," Rudder pressed.

"Well, duh! That's the only way to *get* to the stage door."

Rudder pressed further: "At what time?"

Martha pursed her lips. "Umm . . . about a quarter to eight?"

Who was she asking?

Looming over her, Rudder demanded, "And how long were you gone from the dressing room?"

"Maybe five minutes, tops. You can ask Clara—she was helping me with the costumes."

"Who's Clara?" Rudder asked, checking the names on my list.

I said, "Assistant stage manager. High-school student—an intern."

Rudder's gaze returned to Martha. "Did Clara leave wardrobe during that half hour?"

Martha shook her head. "No. The girl was there when I left for a smoke, and was still there when I got back."

Rudder turned to Brandy for confirmation or denial.

Brandy said, "I didn't see Clara backstage, Sheriff."

Rudder asked, "Martha, then what did you do?"

She shrugged. "Then I left to go watch from the audience."

Rudder snapped his little notebook shut. "All right, then. You can go."

Martha stood, said dramatically, "*Thank* you," a trifle over-the-top for my taste, and left.

The sheriff called for Miguel, who leaned a hand on the interview chair, but did not sit, meeting the law enforcer's gaze head-on.

"I know what questions you've been asking, Sheriff," the handsome man said, rather belligerently. "So let's make this brief. I *was* backstage, and I *did* have access to the maintenance room . . . because I'm the *stage manager*! That doesn't mean I had a damn thing to do with Madeline's death."

As Miguel was heading out, Rudder asked his back, "But you *did* have an affair with her."

Miguel turned, dark eyes flashing. "That's stretching a point. What we're talking about is a one-night stand, which I regret."

I said, "Pardon the interruption, gentlemen . . . but, Miguel, did Madeline threaten to tell Kimberly about your . . . one-night stand?"

"Yes, she did. But I told Kim myself, before Madeline got to her. End of story."

And on that decent curtain line, he left.

Finally Kimberly took the chair.

"Miguel advised me not to talk to you," Kimberly began. She'd been crying, eyes red. "But I . . . I *want* to."

"I appreciate that," Rudder said. "Let's start with who you saw backstage—no matter how briefly—in the half an hour before the play began."

The attractive blonde understudy thought about that. "Well, I *was* there, of course, with Brandy—we were sitting together, just off the wing. Paul came through on his way to fix some stage lights. . . . Martha walked by and went out the stage door, lighting up a cigarette. . . . Leroy was there, getting ready to run the conveyor belt . . . and Miguel came over just to be with me for a while. Then Madeline got into position for her entrance, and Miguel left, then Brandy, and I went over to the prop table and picked up the fruitcake on the platter, then I stood behind Madeline, ready for my first line."

"What about this high-school girl?" Rudder asked. "Clara?"

Kimberly shook her head. "I didn't see her. Did you, Brandy?"

"No."

Rudder asked, "What about the bit players playin' factory workers?"

"They were already onstage," Kimberly answered. "In position for the curtain to rise."

Rudder paced some more, then came to a stop in front of the seated Kimberly. "So then, after Brandy left you, and after Madeline made her entrance . . .. that put you alone with the fruitcake."

"Yes," Kimberly said, barely audible. "I'm afraid it did. There's no one who can prove *my* innocence. But I am innocent."

Rudder said, "You don't deny you knew that your 'friend' Miguel had an affair with the de Morlaye woman?"

"That was before Miguel and I . . ." Her eyes flashed with indignation. "Is there anything else, Sheriff?"

"No. No, that'll be all. For now."

When Kimberly had gone, Rudder looked at me, then Brandy, then me again. "Well, ladies, what do you make of our little cast of characters?"

I rose from the couch. "I think . . . I *know* . . . you have the kind of problem, Sheriff, that no detective relishes."

Brandy, taking Sushi with her, got to her feet as well. She finished my thought, saying: "Too many suspects with means, opportunity, and motive."

My cell phone rang, the screen identifying Virginia Shoemaker. Word had reached the chair of the Playhouse board of directors of Madeline's untimely demise.

"Vivian," the woman said, in that archly theatrical way of hers, "I'll come right to the point. In spite of this terrible tragedy, we all agree that we must go forward with the production. The food pantry is depending on our contribution this Christmas. We simply *can't* let the destitute down."

"No, indeed," I replied somberly, my acting skills masking my joy. My little masterpiece would go on after all!

Virginia was saying, "I realize we may take *some* criticism. . . ." She trailed off, to make way for validation.

And I gave it to her: "My dear Virginia, there may not be a Santa Claus, but there will be a fruitcake play. It's what Madeline would have wanted. Why, I can hear her now up in that great playhouse in the sky, saying, 'The show must go on!' "

Or was it from down below?

"Yes, yes!" Virginia blurted. "Our thoughts precisely. Is the understudy up to the job?"

"I'm quite sure Kimberly will be marvelous."

She would be even better than someone else whose name I won't mention because it's unkind to speak ill of the dead. Particularly the recently dead.

Now, dear reader, you may wonder why I—after coveting the leading role myself—wasn't jumping at the chance to take over. The answer (as another great detective once said) is, it was easy. There was one role in this production I would rather perform than Mrs. Hattie Anne Babcock, and that's Vivian Borne, Sleuth.

"Very good," Virginia said. "Do keep us posted!" And she ended the call.

I turned to the sheriff, who'd been listening to my half of the conversation. "It is *possible,* isn't it? To release the theater from crime scene quarantine?"

Rudder was rubbing his chin. "Might be to our advantage at that. Yes, Vivian, the show can go on."

"Goody goody!"

"Restrain your glee, Mother," Brandy said sourly. Even at Christmastime, she could find a way to be negative! "Do you want me to go find Kimberly?"

"Yes," I ordered. "But let *me* give her the news that though she was going out there an understudy, she's coming back a star . . . suspect."

Act Three

All I Want for Christmas Is a Fruitcake

Brandy back at the helm, and it *was* a tuba.

When Mother informed me that the murder of our leading lady was not going to prevent the show from going on, I was skeptical that we'd have anyone in the opening-night audience, apart from relatives of the cast and crew. Oh, there might be a few ghoulish folks curious to see what the play would be like, now that its star had fallen. I considered such people akin to ambulance chasers, and gawkers lingering near the scene of a crime.

But as curtain time neared, the auditorium began filling up, until hardly an empty seat could be found.

Maybe I'd underestimated the number of

ghouls in Serenity. More likely this solid attendance reflected the show's substantial presale of tickets—if there's anything a Midwesterner hates, it's not getting his or her money's worth.

And, even under these circumstances, no matter who might be filling those seats and why, I'm sure all of us involved in the production were pleased to have a capacity house.

Yesterday, upon first hearing of the decision to go on with *The Fruitcake That Saved Christmas,* Kimberly had been reluctant, though admitting she was well prepared to step into Madeline's role.

Mother, along with Miguel, worked to convince her otherwise.

"Dear," Mother said, "you must put aside your personal feelings. Think of everyone, including yourself, who have put their all into this production. Think of the food pantry and those it serves. Think of the tradition of our annual Playhouse Christmas production."

"I . . . I just don't think I *can,*" the understudy replied.

"Kim, please," Miguel said, facing her, taking her by the arms. "No matter what the circumstances, it's a once-in-a-lifetime opportunity. You'll be *wonderful* in the part."

Kimberly blanched. "It's not about me being 'wonderful,' Miguel—and it's 'once in a lifetime' only because of a death. Shouldn't we try to do the respectful thing?"

His cheeks flushed. "Do you think that diva would have hesitated stepping in, if the circumstances had been reversed?"

Her eyes flared, and she broke away from Miguel. "Stop it! All of you. I won't be manipulated! It doesn't matter that we didn't like Madeline. She was murdered—on the very stage you want me to perform on! Maybe I should hit my mark and stand in the chalk body outline!"

"There won't be one, dear," Mother said. "That's not a procedure that Sheriff Rudder employs."

"I was just trying to make a point!"

Mother surreptitiously waved a hand to Miguel to stay back, then said soothingly, "I'm afraid as a director I do have a manipulative streak, and I do apologize if I drifted into the area of bad taste. The decision is yours." She sighed. "Of course, if we don't go on, the less fortunate here in Serenity will have to do without a Christmas dinner. There's always next year!"

Good thing Mother was restraining her urge to be manipulative.

Blatant though that had been, Kimberly fell silent.

Mother and I exchanged glances. Miguel was studying the actress, his look tortured.

"All right, all right," Kimberly said, shaking her head, the corn silk locks bouncing. "I'll do it. But only because it's for charity." Then she added, her voice breaking, "And because . . . because *something* good has to come out of this."

Mother patted the understudy's arm. "Thank you, dear. I felt sure you'd do the right thing."

Definition of "the right thing": what Mother wants.

Still, my first reaction was to think how brave Kimberly was. My second was to think that, if she turned out to be the killer, that had been a Tony-worthy performance. . . .

And so, here it was, opening night, nearly curtain time. I was backstage, standing in the stage-right wing, not letting either fruitcake out of my sight. I was not about to allow a repeat performance of yesterday's fatal dress rehearsal.

Clara, next to me, dressed in a drab factory costume, was saying, "I just can't wrap my head around this."

I glanced at her. Mother had given Kimberly's role of the cook to the intern. Clara seemed both happy and terrified.

I said, "Around what, honey?"

"That I'm actually *in* a play. Even *our* high-school productions? Always backstage."

I smiled. "That's where *I* like it."

The girl turned her plump face to me, some prettiness rising out of the plain features thanks to stage makeup. "I'm just so nervous, Brandy. I studied and studied my lines all afternoon. But what if I forget them?"

"You'll be fine," I told her. "And if you do 'go up,' as we say in the thea-tah, I'll be right here to feed 'em to you."

"You're the best, Brandy."

As the orchestra began the overture, Clara took my hand, holding it tightly, and I gave it a reassuring squeeze.

As it happened, Clara was letter perfect, and quite believable as a cook fond of fruitcakes.

Not that it took anything away from Kimberly,

who really stole the show. She gave Hattie Ann Babcock a more sensitive, realistic reading than Madeline's tough-businesswoman's interpretation. If she lacked the late actress's showbiz savvy, Kimberly had charm to spare. The audience loved her, and when she came out for her curtain call bow, she got a standing ovation, and enthusiastic applause from the rest of the company.

Peeking out, I could see the fruitcake in the audience—that is, Mother—in her aisle seat in the first row (Sushi on her lap), looking ecstatic. Her play was a hit, and she couldn't have been happier—unless she'd played the lead herself.

After the curtain had come down for the last time, an ebullient cast and crew congratulated each other, buoyed by the audience's reaction.

For a few moments, the death on this very stage was forgotten.

But when Sheriff Rudder strode into this happy tableau, it came immediately back to everyone's mind.

"Well, Sheriff," Mother chirped, "what did you think of our little production? Did it get you into a festive mood?"

"Just got here, Vivian. Didn't see it."

Mother's expression could not have been more startled and offended had he thrown cold water in her face.

Snippily, she asked, "Then why did you bother coming here at all?"

"Because, Vivian, I have a job to do. You're in charge here, right? The director? Well, I want to see the following people—Paul, Martha, Miguel, Clara, Kimberly, and Leroy. Right now."

Mother asked, "You mean in the dressing room?"

He shook his head. "No. Center stage is as good a place as any to act this out. Rest of you can leave!"

When the bit players and stagehands had departed, Rudder addressed the remaining little group gathered together in a semicircle right around the spot where Madeline had taken her last, unintentional bow.

With his back to the closed curtain, the sheriff said, "I'm sorry to have to detain you folks again, but we have some new information in this investigation."

Kimberly blurted, "Sheriff, let everyone else go!"

"Excuse me, young lady?"

"I'm . . . I'm the one who poisoned the fruitcake."

There were gasps from the rest of the suspects. Mother, ever the director, raised a cautionary hand, stopping any of her people from saying anything more.

Kimberly, her face firmly set, continued, "It was selfish of me to go on tonight. So horribly selfish. When they were all applauding, I felt awful. Terrible. So *guilty.*"

Miguel began to speak but Mother shook her head at him and he paused.

Kimberly explained: "I lied to myself and said I was only going on because this event was for charity. But in my heart I knew I took Madeline's place for selfish reasons. I don't care what it leads to—I have to take responsibility for my actions."

Miguel stepped forward, shaking his head, no restraining gesture from Mother this time.

"Kim," he said. "You don't have to lie." He turned to Rudder. "She's just trying to protect me. *I* poisoned the fruitcake."

"No, Sheriff!" Kimberly said, eyes wild. "He's trying to protect *me*!" She gazed at Miguel, her expression tragic. "Do you think I could live with letting you take the blame for my actions?"

Rudder patted the air with both hands. "All right, you two, enough. Who's telling the truth?"

"I believe they *both* are, Sheriff," Mother said, stepping forward. "If without the other's knowledge . . ."

I had to agree—Kimberly was a good actress, but Miguel was no actor at all, and their heartfelt performance seemed sincere.

"Oh no," Kimberly gasped, staring at Miguel. "Did you . . . ? Did you do it, *too*? Oh, my God, what have we done?" She covered her face with her hands.

An equally stricken Miguel looked at Rudder. "We were just joking around the other night, saying, wouldn't it serve Madeline right if she missed opening night and you went on instead? We joked about how just a little sprinkling of that rat poison would make her sick. Only, I started thinking it could *really* work, and Kim could go out there for Madeline, you know, and really shine. Then, after Brandy put the fruitcakes on the prop table, when I walked by? I . . .

sprinkled a little of that rat poison on the fruitcake for Madeline."

Kimberly wore an expression of horror. "I did the same thing! Just before I carried the fruitcake onstage. Just sprinkled a little on. I didn't, I swear to God, I *never* meant for her to die!"

Miguel turned to Kimberly, taking both her hands in his. "Neither one of us meant for Madeline to get anything but sick. But the combination of what we both did. . . . It was a kind of accident! We're not murderers."

Mother said, rather clinically, "More like manslaughter, wouldn't you say, Sheriff?"

Throughout this emotional confession, I had been studying Rudder, who seemed detached during such important revelations, which puzzled me.

At least I was puzzled till he said, "Madeline *didn't* die from rat poison. She died from arsenic."

Paul frowned. "Arsenic?"

Martha asked, "Where would any of us get arsenic?"

Janitor Leroy jerked a thumb over his shoulder. "Outta the maintenance room."

Clara said, "You mean . . . there wasn't just rat poison on top? There was poison *in* the fruitcake, too?"

"Nope," Rudder said, shaking his head. "No poison baked in, and what was on top wouldn't have been enough to do the trick. Just make her sick, like you two kids thought. That fruitcake may have saved Christmas, but it didn't kill your leading lady."

Everyone was taking this in with shocked expressions, except Mother, who said, "And you know this how, Sheriff?"

"Vivian, during the preliminary autopsy this afternoon, the doc did something called the Marsh test, which shows a fatal dose of arsenic was absorbed through the skin."

Kimberly, smiling although in a hysterical fashion, said, "Then . . . then Miguel and I *didn't* kill her."

"No," Rudder said. "You may have acted like rats, but you didn't poison her . . . not to death, anyway."

She and Miguel hugged each other, though neither looked exactly happy.

Mother asked, "Sheriff, what *part* of Madeline's skin absorbed the arsenic?"

"That would be her face."

I asked, "How long would it take before . . ."

"It killed her?" Rudder finished. "Probably an hour or so."

Mother had been fiddling with her cell phone, and now she moved next to Rudder.

"Shortly after the murder," Mother said, "I took photos of Madeline's dressing room." She held up the cell and let him see its screen. "This is a picture of the dressing table."

"Yeah?" Rudder asked. "And?"

"Her liquid makeup bottle is missing."

Rudder frowned, but he was nodding. "Which could be how the arsenic got on her face—in the makeup!"

"Almost certainly," Mother replied. "And since that makeup always remained in her dressing room, it would have been easy for someone to have tampered with it."

I said, "Mother, since Madeline left her dressing room at five minutes to eight, and died about eight-fifteen, who here had the opportunity to retrieve the damning bottle?"

Mother smiled in her best cat-that-ate-the-canary fashion. "I think I can determine that right now, dear."

While the others exchanged glances, Mother walked downstage to the closed curtain where Rudder faced the suspects, positioned herself beside the sheriff, and pointed a finger at Paul. "*You* were in the lighting booth between the time Madeline left her dressing room and collapsed onstage."

Startled, Paul said, "So what?"

"So . . . you're in the clear."

The finger moved on to Martha. "*You* were seated in the audience. You're in the clear."

The finger next found Leroy. "*You* were operating the conveyor belt backstage. You're in the clear."

The finger sought out Kimberly. "*You* were in the wing, standing behind Madeline. In the clear."

The finger trained on Miguel. "And you? From my seat in the front row, I could see you standing in the stage-left wing. Also in the clear."

Finally the finger settled on Clara. "But, *you*, dear, were in the wardrobe room, just a few steps away from Madeline's dressing room. It would have been child's play for you to retrieve the makeup bottle, which you'd laced with arsenic sometime before Madeline had arrived for rehearsal. What did you do with it, dear? Throw it in the Dumpster out back? Or toss it out your car window into a cornfield? No matter. The sheriff will find the bottle . . . and your fingerprints on it."

Clara's face had a bisque-baby blankness. ". . . Can I still be in Saturday's matinee?"

"I'm afraid not, dear," Mother replied, almost kindly. "But all in all, yours has been a remarkable performance."

Rudder took the girl's arm. She was sobbing quietly now, tears streaming. "Clara, you'll have to go with me to the county jail. You can call your parents from there."

Then he led the intern off the stage.

"Imagine," I said, "that harmless-looking kid killing somebody."

"*Madeline* killed Madeline," Mother said, colder than cold cream. "You see, dear, she could act many a part. But one key role eluded her."

That was my cue. "What role is that, Mother?"

"Being a decent human being offstage."

Curtain Call

I'll Be Home for Fruitcake

Mother has requested that I turn the rest of this narrative over to her. She quite reasonably pointed out that I was not present for the coda of this piece, and why should the reader get the story secondhand? Anyway, it's almost Christmas, and this was a gift Mother really wanted, and it doesn't cost me a dime.

You might wish to have a cup of eggnog before pressing on. The kind of eggnog Captain Morgan likes!

Yes, it is I, Vivian Borne, director and playwright of *The Fruitcake That Saved Christmas,* which should soon be available from Samuel French publishers (they haven't gotten back to me just yet). And I do appreciate Brandy passing the baton or perhaps the pen (or computer?), since from here on out, this is really a one-woman show.

No, come to think of it, it's a two-hander. I did have a key supporting player.

You see, after Clara's arraignment, Sheriff Rudder was kind enough to allow me to visit the troubled girl in the county jail, where she was awaiting trial.

Sidebar: In recent years I worked tirelessly as a community leader in support of a new downtown jail—and we now have one, a state-of-the-art, no-barbwire facility that looks more like your average medical clinic. Those who accuse me of having an ulterior motive may have a point: I did land in the old bug-infested hoosegow once or twice. (Once was for chaining myself to a wrecking ball about to demolish one of Serenity's Victorian buildings; twice was for driving with a suspended license. There may be a thrice, but it escapes me.)

Midmorning, with sun finding its way through the crosshatch of wires on high windows, I sat in the little visitation cubicle across from Clara, a Plexiglas window separating us. I was wearing another Breckenridge outfit (pink sweater, winter-white slacks); Clara was less fashionable in standard-issue jumpsuit of bright orange, a color that did nothing for her.

A female guard named Patty (an acquaintance I'd made on recent incarcerations) (listing the reasons would be a pointless digression) loomed behind the girl, but at enough of a distance to give us some privacy. As usual, the woman wore the bored expression of someone who'd been too long on the job. Isn't it sad when someone doesn't love her or his work?

"How are you, dear?" I asked Clara, speaking into the little microphone in the glass (a big improvement over the old jailhouse phones).

"Not bad," the girl said with a shrug, seemingly unconcerned about her future.

"Are they treating you well?"

I'd quite enjoyed all of *my* stays.

She perked up. "Oh yes. And the food isn't half-bad." She might have been a child reporting what life at an upscale camp was like.

"You'll want to avoid the meat loaf," I advised. "They go overboard with the filler." I had gained five pounds during my last incarceration.

I continued: "Dear, do you mind if we speak of the . . . unpleasantness?"

She frowned just a little.

"Dear, anything you tell me will be in *strictest* confidence, I assure you."

Clara's cheerfulness faded, and she stared down at her lap. "I . . . I'd rather not."

"I may be able to help you."

"I have a lawyer."

A court-appointed lawyer of no renown.

"I still think I can help, dear."

Her eyes met mine. "How?"

"Let's just converse and see. Now. In one of your backstage conversations with Brandy, you mentioned being on an antidepressant. Or so Brandy reports."

Clara nodded. "That's right. Because I was having a hard time at school."

"Teased, dear? Bullied?"

She nodded. "But after I started working at the Playhouse, my doctor said I was doing so well that he took me off the meds." She shrugged again. "He said he didn't want me using 'em as a crutch."

"Does your lawyer know of this?"

"No. I didn't see what it had to do with anything."

"It has everything to do with anything. It's vital that your lawyer be informed of this."

"Why?" Dull eyes momentarily brightened. "You mean, it could get me off?"

"No. But it might lead to a reduced sentence, or even affect the type of institution where you make your amends."

She winced and said, "It was just spur-of-the-moment, you know."

Actually it was quite premeditated, but I said, "Because Madeline was so cruel to you?"

"She was awful. Called me fat and a pig and stupid. And I admired her so!"

"Tell me, dear—how did you know that adding arsenic to Madeline's makeup would have the effect it did? Did you read it in a book? Agatha Christie, perhaps?"

I hated to lay a real murder at the Grand Dame of Mystery's feet, but it could make for a good argument in court.

Clara shook her head. "Madeline told me."

"*What?* Explain!"

The girl nodded. "It's funny. At first, she was

nice to me, and let me hang around her dressing room before rehearsals. One time, when I said how pretty her complexion was, she told me that in the olden days women would put a little arsenic in their face cream to make their skin whiter. But they had to be careful not to use too much because it could kill them." Clara shrugged with her eyebrows. "So, in a way, it was kind of Madeline's fault, wasn't it, really?"

So—the diva had directed her own final performance.

"Dear," I said, "Madeline may have given you the idea, but *you* put it into effect. Make no mistake about it—you took another person's life."

Clara's eyes welled. "I know. I wish I could undo it . . . but I can't."

She had a box of tissues on her side of the Plexiglas and used several.

I waited for a while, then said, "I don't know what the outcome of your trial will be, Clara, but if you find yourself inside for a while? Keep in mind it's what you do during that time that can make a difference in your life. Because someday you *will* get out into the world again."

Clara wiped her nose on her sleeve. "Like do what on the inside?"

And I told her about how I had, on a fairly recent visit, formed a jailhouse repertory company with the other female inmates, and that we put on plays—first for ourselves, then the male inmates, and finally, the general public.

(I left out the part about two of the girls doing a runner on an off-campus performance, which put an end to our theater group. Also, I felt it best not to mention that the play they skipped out during was *Arsenic and Old Lace.*)

"Dear," I said, bringing enthusiasm to my voice, "just think of it! *You* could be the lead actress in the new jailhouse theater group."

"I . . . I could?"

"But of course! You were marvelous as the cook. Completely believable. Why, I wouldn't be surprised if, after you pay your debt to society, you might make a name for yourself on the Great White Way."

This was horse hockey right out of my production of *My Fair Lady,* but the girl did need encouragement.

Her eyes were shining like new pennies, Lincoln side out. "You *really* think so?"

"Why, after the experience you'll get with the new theater group . . . certainly! Silver lining."

The sullen Patty said, "Time."

Standing, Clara asked, "You'll come to the trial?"

I beamed at her. "Wouldn't miss it for the world. I'll be testifying, you know."

"And I know you'll be just wonderful," the girl said, smiling back. "Thank you, Mrs. Borne, for caring about me. My folks are pretty mad at me right now. You know something?"

"Dear?"

"That wasn't the fruitcake that saved Christmas at all. Anyway, it sure ruined mine."

And Patty escorted her out.

Now, dear reader, before you put me up alongside Mother Teresa, I should reveal that behind my interest in Clara was my own ulterior motive.

I had a drawerful of plays I'd written that the board hadn't deemed good enough for the Playhouse, but that might well see the light of day inside the county jail. Silver lining indeed—pure tinsel.

Look out, Samuel French!

A block from the facility, I caught the gas-powered trolley. At home, where I was greeted by the aroma of a freshly baked fruitcake. Of course, the truth is I generally don't like fruitcake—but that antique recipe of Hattie's is really not too shabby!

As I entered our retro 1950s red-and-white kitchen, Brandy was removing a piping-hot example from the oven, with Sushi dancing in anticipation nearby.

"How'd it go with Clara?" she asked.

"I'll tell you all about it over a slice of fruitcake and some hot tea."

Soon we were seated at the antique Duncan Phyfe dining-room table, where I filled Brandy in.

Brandy, on her second piece (a new convert to fruitcake, at least the Hattie variety) said, "Did Clara tell you *why* she killed Madeline?"

"We spoke of it," I said, sneaking Sushi a bite under the table. "But in no great detail."

Because I hadn't needed to.

Brandy said, "Pretty obvious Clara had idolized Madeline. Maybe the girl even had a crush on her."

"Possibly," I said. "But when the object of her affection became the purveyor of her affliction, an unmedicated Clara took her revenge."

Brandy nodded, took another bite.

I helped myself to another slice. A little matter like murder was not about to put me off this delectable Christmas treat.

And now you, dear reader, can enjoy it, too.

The Serenity Factory Fruitcake

3 cups pecans, coarsely chopped
1 lb. pitted dates, coarsely chopped
1 cup halved maraschino cherries
¾ cup flour
¾ cup sugar
½ tsp. baking powder
½ tsp. salt
3 eggs
1 tsp. vanilla extract
(rat poison optional)

In a large bowl combine nuts, dates, and cherries; add in flour, sugar, baking powder and salt, and mix well. In a small bowl, beat eggs until foamy, stir in vanilla, then fold into main mixture, mixing well. Pour into greased 9"x5" loaf pan. Bake at 300 degrees for 1 hour and 45 minutes, or until inserted toothpick comes out clean. Cool before removing from pan.

A Trash 'n' Treasures Tip

Collecting vintage recipes is not only fun, but a glimpse into the past. The best place to find old recipes is at an estate sale of an elderly person. But don't restrict yourself to out-of-print cookbooks or the typical household recipe tin; newspaper clippings and manufacturer's pamphlets of kitchen gadgets can also be a good source for unique dishes. Some 1950s and early '60s magazine-style cookbooks have wonderful photos of "unfortunate foods." Our mutual advice, re: fruitcake recipes in such publications, is to beware—the more colorful the cake, the less tasty the outcome.

Antiques St. Nicked

Brandy's quote:
"If you want to keep a secret
you also must hide it from yourself."

—George Orwell

Mother's quote:
"There is something about a closet
that makes a skeleton terribly restless."

—John Barrymore

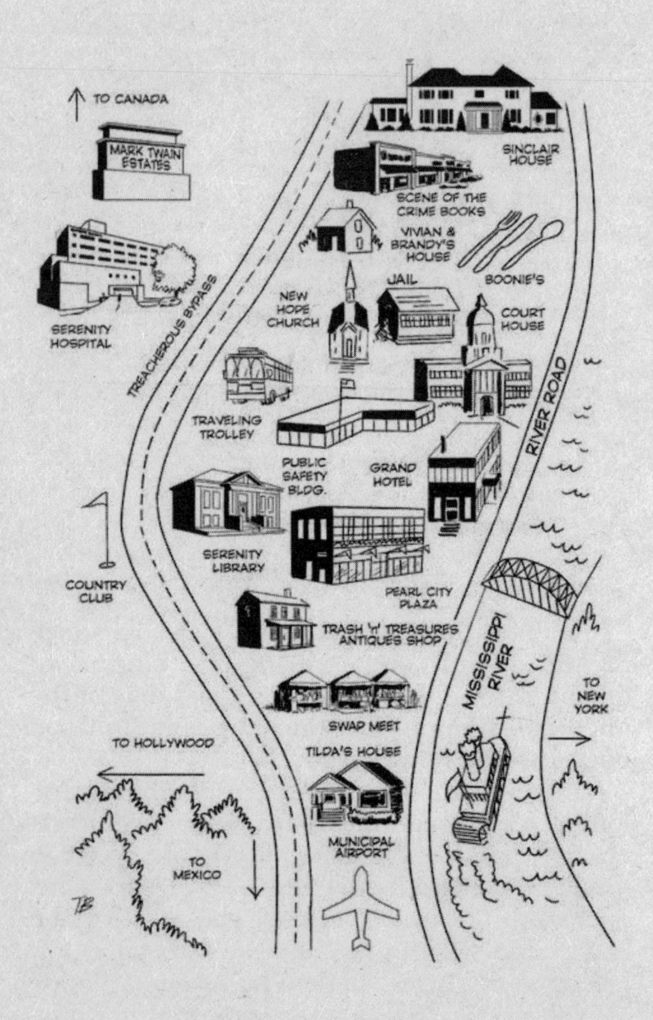

TO CANADA
MARK TWAIN ESTATES
SINCLAIR HOUSE
SCENE OF THE CRIME BOOKS
VIVIAN & BRANDY'S HOUSE
BOONIE'S
SERENITY HOSPITAL
TREACHEROUS BYPASS
NEW HOPE CHURCH
JAIL
COURT HOUSE
RIVER ROAD
TRAVELING TROLLEY
PUBLIC SAFETY BLDG.
GRAND HOTEL
SERENITY LIBRARY
COUNTRY CLUB
PEARL CITY PLAZA
TRASH 'N' TREASURES ANTIQUES SHOP
MISSISSIPPI RIVER
TO NEW YORK
SWAP MEET
TO HOLLYWOOD
TILDA'S HOUSE
MUNICIPAL AIRPORT
TO MEXICO
TB

Chapter One

"Up on the housetop reindeer paws,
out jumps good old Santa Claus . . ."

Today was the first Saturday in December, which meant only one thing to the citizens of quaint little Serenity, Iowa, on the banks of the Mighty Mississippi—the annual Holiday Stroll had once again arrived.

This evening the downtown merchants, following their usual nine-to-five hours, would reopen from seven to nine, luring shoppers in from the cold with free cups of hot chocolate, steaming cider, and homemade cookies, all in the name of good cheer (and early holiday sales).

Every storefront window had some yuletide display, from religious (manger scene) to whimsical (teddy bears), not to mention collectible (Department 56 miniature villages). Even ol' sourpuss Mrs. Hunter, who with her husband ran the hardware store, applied festive red and green bows to the tools arranged in their window.

Outdoor events went on as well. Each street corner had something going, whether a choir singing familiar carols or a small brass band playing holiday favorites, and of course, the customary Salvation Army red kettle with volunteer bell-ringer.

Ever since I was little, Mother would take me to the Holiday Stroll—Mother being Vivian Borne, seventies (actual age her well-guarded secret), bipolar, widowed, Danish stock, local thespian, antiques store co-owner, and self-styled amateur sleuth; and me being Brandy Borne, thirty-three, Prozac-prone (since returning to live with Mother after my divorce), co-owner of our antiques store, and frequent reluctant accomplice in Mother's detecting escapades.

(Clearly if you object to parenthetical asides, you have chosen the wrong Christmas story.)

Our Trash 'n' Treasures antiques shop, located at the foot of the downtown, was not among the businesses opening their doors tonight. We'd participated in last year's Stroll to less than merry results—namely, one smashed Mary Gregory green glass pitcher, one stolen pipe commemorating Charles Lindbergh's 1927 solo transatlantic flight, and a solitary sale (a twenty-dollar Keane print of a crying big-eyed waif).

Accompanying Mother and me tonight—but no less bundled up against the cold—was Sushi, my diabetic shih tzu. Soosh was wearing a leopard-print dog blanket with matching booties that she kept trying to kick off. I had on a black military-style jacket, black leather gloves, and a red wool scarf longer than Harry Potter's. Mother had donned an old raccoon coat that looked like something Andy Hardy wore in one of his college boolah-boolah movies. Thank goodness she only dragged it out of mothballs for the bitterest of winter days (or when she went off her meds, which was an indicator of same) (if it wasn't cold out, that is).

(*Mother to Brandy:* Dear, I know you took a creative writing class at the community college some years ago, but regarding those last two sentences, please try to be more concise. Our readers expect a higher literary standard after nine books and two novellas.)

(*Brandy to Mother:* Not if they've read them they don't.)

Anyway, the Stroll was already in full swing as Mother and I—Sushi in my arms so she wouldn't get trod on—made our way along the crowded downtown sidewalks, our breaths pluming, our boots adding more tracks in the lightly falling snow.

First stop, per usual, was to see Santa and Rudolph, who were always at the outdoor plaza of the First National Bank. If the Holiday Stroll was a Serenity tradition, this particular Santa (and his very special helper) was a Holiday Stroll tradition.

Simon Wright had been playing Jolly Old St. Nick every Holiday Stroll since I was in elementary school, and even though I was no longer a wonderment-filled child, there remained something comforting about seeing Simon year after year in his velvet red suit with white fur cuffs, black belt, and convincing (if fake) white beard, seated in a thronelike red chair in front of a wooden storage shed transformed into a pretend toy workshop.

The workshop—a sign above the door proclaimed it as such—was a colorful gingerbread house with silhouettes of elves painted on the windows. But what set Simon's setup apart from, say, a regular mall Santa was his actual, no fooling, really real reindeer penned nearby and tied to a post.

And for a donation to Simon's pet cause—the construction of a new shelter for domestic violence victims—the kiddies could have their picture taken near Rudolph, whose un-red nose was explained by Santa as only glowing red in flight on Christmas Eve.

(I snapped a free one with my cell phone.)

As we approached the bank plaza, Mother waved a hand, calling out, "Oh, *yoo*-hoo, Simon! I mean *Santa!* It's your favorite non-elf helper—*Viv-i-an!*"

Simon Wright barely afforded her a glance, and Mother's upraised hand went limp.

Seeing her hurt expression, I said, "Now, Mother—Santa *is* busy with that long line of kids who're even younger than you."

"He's never been too busy for me before," she muttered, adjusting her oversize, somewhat magnifying glasses.

Simon was a semiretired farmer who kept various animals—ponies, goats, sheep, even llama (and, of course, the reindeer)—to take to county fairs as a petting zoo.

After she'd been a widow for some years, Mother and widower Simon had gone out for a time. Of course, little Brandy would have loved to have Santa as her new father—think of the year-round presents! But Mother liked her freedom and discouraged any move toward matrimony from any suitor, even Santa Claus. Apparently the only role local diva Vivian Borne did not care to play was Mrs. Claus.

They had remained good, warm friends nonetheless.

I'd been watching Rudolph and commented, "That reindeer seems . . . agitated. Don't you think?" In the past, the animal had always been quite placid in his job.

"These children *are* quite noisy," Mother replied, then brightened. "Simon must be worried about the animal! That would explain the frosty reception for yours truly."

"You're probably right. I hope Rudolph doesn't get spooked. That's a big animal."

But Mother was still thinking about Santa's slight. "Well . . . perhaps we'll come back later and give Simon a proper Christmas greeting."

Sushi squirmed in my arms. "Rudolph isn't the only beast getting agitated," I said. "Our little angel here wants to go to the p-e-t store, and if I don't take her, she'll just keep after me. You coming?"

Mother seemed distracted. "I'll catch up with you later, dear. . . . I've just spotted some of my Red-Hatted League gal pals."

The League was a mystery book club off-shoot of the Red Hat Society.

Sushi gave a sharp, impatient bark. *On Brandy! On Vivian! Dash away! Dash away all!*

Paws and Claws, located on the main floor of a restored redbrick Victorian building, was run by Alura Winters, a petite woman in her late twenties who might have been a woodland sprit with those green eyes, that translucent skin, and her flowing red hair tucked behind elfin ears.

The pets who accompanied their owners (or was that vice versa?) loved Alura because each got a free treat (the pets, not the owners), and Paws and Claws seemed to be one place where all the animals could get along—cats with other cats, dogs with other dogs, even cats with dogs (to paraphrase Bill Murray).

Was this magical animal kingdom due to Alura's loving aura? Not hardly—*behave yourself Rover or Tabby, or no treat!*

Animals learn fast when it comes to their stomachs.

I put Sushi down so she could wander around the store while I picked out a gift for her—a squirrel with no stuffing whose squeaker was not accessible by a Velcro opening (I learn pretty fast, too). Still, at the mercy of Sushi's sharp little teeth, the cloth toy would only last till maybe New Year's Eve.

Alura employed an older woman to run the cash register so she herself could be free to mingle with customers and dispense treats to well-behaved pets. After a few minutes, I saw an opening to speak to her.

"Say," I asked, "did Simon get a new reindeer?"

To my knowledge there had been two other Rudolphs, reindeer having a life span similar to a dog or cat.

The elfin features frowned in thought. "No, I don't think so. I'm pretty sure it's the same one . . . why?"

"I just thought the animal was acting a little . . . off."

"How so?"

I shrugged. "Irritable? Anxious? Skittish?"

She returned the shrug. "I took Rudy an apple earlier, when Simon was setting up, and he seemed just fine then." She paused, then added, "But maybe the children are starting to bother him—he *is* getting up there in age."

I smirked. "Simon or Rudolph?"

Her laugh was a Tinkerbell tinkle. "Well, both. But I don't suppose *Simon* was acting skittish."

"Well, he did ignore Mother's 'yoo-hoo.' And they used to be an item."

"Maybe he was just staying in character. An actress of Vivian's caliber should understand that."

"Good point," I said.

On my way to the cash register, I ran into a middle-aged man with wispy white hair and thick wire-framed glasses that reduced his eyes to raisins. What his full name was I couldn't tell you, but everybody called him Dumpster Dan, a harmless soul who lived a few blocks away in the old YMCA, which been converted into housing for indigents and those fleeing domestic violence.

"Hello, Dan," I said with a smile. "Merry early Christmas."

"Merry Christmas to you, Miz Borne!" He wore a rumpled trench coat with similarly wrinkled slacks beneath and dirty tennis shoes. He did not exactly smell like a candy cane, but otherwise was a pleasant presence.

Occasionally Dan came into our antiques shop with something "precious" that he'd found in a Dumpster. And, due to his less-than-stellar financial status, we usually bought the item no matter how un-precious it might be.

Dan gave me a big, multicolored grin. "Wonderful turnout for the Stroll, isn't it?" He cupped his hand to his mouth so no one would overhear, then whispered excitedly, "Boy, the Dumpsters'll be overflowin' by the end of the night."

"Like a stocking Christmas morning," I said.

"I'm *sure* to find something of value for you and your mother."

"Well, if you do, feel free to stop by the shop."

"Oh I will, I will!"

I moved on to the cash register and, after making my purchase, found Sushi in the dog-food aisle, confabbing with a miniature schnauzer. On the way out of the store, she tried to wrangle a second treat from Alura, and succeeded due to the general Christmas spirit, but possibly setting a bad precedent.

Sushi and I made several other stops for gifts.

At Artists' Alley I bought Mother a piece of pottery that she collected (support your local artisans!), and at Meerdink's Men's Clothiers I got my special guy a navy sweater; and at the Hall Tree, I bought myself a present, a black cashmere sweater, just in case Mother's gift to me was a dud.

Final stop was the gourmet popcorn store, which made the most delicious caramel corn along with a dozen other flavors; the cagey owners piped the delicious aromas outside, so only someone with a terminally stuffed-up nose could resist and walk on by.

Many of the shops had either entertainment, live Christmas music of some sort, or free food stuffs, most often Christmas cookies and punch. I had to reluctantly avoid most of these seasonal temptations or Sushi would have begged for samples with a diabetic catastrophe in the offing.

By the time I'd finished shopping, the Stroll was winding down. Most of the outside events—choirs, bands, and bell-ringers—had already dispersed because the snow was coming down heavier, the wind gaining some bite.

I called Mother on my cell, and she texted me to meet her at Simon's display. So I trudged the four blocks through gathering snow, carrying Sushi along with my packages (she'd managed to lose all but one bootie) (why do we humans insist on trying to clothe canines?).

Arriving at Simon's stand at the same time as Mother, we found the throne empty, a sign on the chair reading, "SANTA IS CHECKING ON HIS ELVES." A forlorn-looking Rudolph stood with his magnificently antlered head bowed against the blustery wind.

Mother said, "It's not like Simon to close before the Stroll is officially over."

I set Sushi down. "Who could blame him?" I shivered. "It's getting *nasty* cold." The last word came out "told."

"Dear, remember—neither rain nor snow nor sleet!"

"That's mail carriers, Mother, not Santa. And that hasn't been true for *them* for yuh-yuh-yuh-yuh-years."

Sushi, kicking off a final bootie, trotted over to the reindeer and barked. The caribou lifted its massive head with rack of horns and made a sound more suited to a pig oinking.

Soosh then trotted over to the workshop shed and began scratching at the door.

Now I might have gone over and snatched Sushi up into my arms and scolded her; but the dog had instincts that rivaled the two human sleuths in the family.

So we went over and Mother pushed open the door. Using the small but powerful light on my key chain, I mini-light-sabered around the dark interior . . .

. . . illuminating Simon, in full Santa regalia, sprawled on his back, eyes staring upward, unblinking.

Mother knelt over him, fingers going to his throat.

"Oh dear," I said. "Is it a heart attack?"

She shook her head, then held up fingers coated in red. "No, a different sort of attack altogether."

I gasped just as she sighed, saying, "I'm afraid this good man has been murdered."

Like the Ghost of Christmas Future pointing to Scrooge's tombstone, Mother gestured with bloody fingers to a hammer lying on the floor, its head covered in a red just a little darker than the Santa suit.

"Why would someone kill Simon?" I asked.

But I feared I knew the all-too-mundane answer: for the monetary contents of the red velvet donation bag discarded near the murdered man's feet, the pouch turned inside out, as if Santa had already handed out each and every present.

Chapter Two

"Here is a hammer and lots of tacks,
also a ball and a whip that cracks . . ."

The first responder to my 911 call was Officer Mia Cordona, dark haired, early thirties, with curves not entirely concealed by unisex slacks and a bulky blue jacket.

Mother and I had a somewhat tumultuous history with my one-time friend Mia ever since we'd unintentionally blown her cover on a drug case (we were investigating an unrelated murder, needless to say without Mia's official status).

Anyway, Officer Cordona was clearly not infused with holiday cheer upon seeing the two of us standing in the snow outside Santa's workshop.

"Mia, dear," Mother began, as the law enforcer approached, "might I remind you that this is a crime scene? I realize murder isn't your specialty."

Mia's cheeks, red from the cold wind, turned a deeper, not-at-all Christmassy crimson. "Might I remind you two to stay the hell out of my way?"

Mother tsk-tsked. "Profanity is both unprofessional and unbecoming in a public servant . . . a public servant whose salary we help *pay*, I might add."

Hoping to defuse the tension, I stepped between them, and asked Mia, "Where *should* we go? We did discover the body, and call it in."

Her dark eyes shifted coldly to me. "Go. Home."

Mother's eyebrows climbed over the rims of her big-lensed glasses. "What about our statements?"

"Someone will get them later . . . now *leave*."

"Don't you even want to know—"

"No."

And Mia headed to the shed door.

Mother looked crushed, but as for me, I was fine with not loitering in this nasty (and getting nastier) weather, much less cooling our heels in a clammy, cold interview room at the police station.

Handing Sushi over to Mother, I gathered my packages, which I'd removed from the workshop, and soon Serenity's two most notorious amateur sleuths were walking to their car in decidedly unfestive silence.

At home, in our Victorian-appointed living room, I took my time curling up on the couch with Sushi—it takes a lot of pillows to get comfy on a Queen Anne—while Mother went into the 1950s-style kitchen to make us some tea.

Last year Mother had come up with a nontraditional way of putting up our Christmas tree—and I do mean "putting up." After seeing one Tannenbaum hanging upside down in a floral shop, she did that very thing with ours only to have it come crashing down one winter night, startling us from our wee little beds, shattering a host of glass ornaments.

This year, with reinforced hooks, Mother had our tree hanging sideways (with new plastic ornaments).

Bearing two steaming cups of tea, Mother returned, handed me one, then sat beside me.

I eyed her closely. "How are you doing? I mean, I know you and Simon were . . . close."

"Why I'm fine, dear," Mother replied, sipping her tea.

She has always been able to compartmentalize—perhaps in part a result of her medication—and I already knew her focus was on finding Simon's killer. While she had a sentimental side, Mother also displayed a nearly cold-blooded attitude where death was concerned. To Mother, death was just a part of life.

Car headlights stroked across the front picture window as a vehicle pulled into our drive. With a murmur of a growl, Sushi jumped down from the couch to investigate, and I followed suit, going to the vestibule and opening the front door.

"It's Tony," I said, surprised that the officer

sent to take our statements was the Chief of Police himself; but then, Tony Cassato was that "special guy" of mine I referred to earlier.

As he came in, in his standard top-cop attire—light blue shirt, navy tie, gray slacks under an open topcoat—I felt my eyes fill with tears, my medication not providing the emotional filter of Mother's.

"Are you all right?" Tony asked with concern. In his midforties, he was about six foot, barrel-chested, square-jawed, with military short hair just beginning to gray at the temples.

"Who would kill Santa," I sniffed, sounding like little Brandy of yore, "for a few measly dollars?"

Tony placed his hands on my shoulders and squeezed just a little. "There are some bad people in this world, Brandy—you know that as well as anybody. But trust me—we're making a list, and we'll be checking it more than twice."

"What about all his animals?"

"Animal Control has arranged with a farmer neighbor of his to look after them for now."

Taking my arm gently, he steered me over to the couch, next to Mother, who asked cheerfully, "Would you like some tea, Chief Cassato?"

"No thank you, Vivian." He sat in a needlepoint Queen Anne armchair next to us, which was about as comfortable as a coach-class airplane seat.

Sushi jumped into her favorite man's lap and he gave her a few fond strokes, then, all business, set her back down on the floor where she dutifully curled in a ball at his feet.

Tony removed a little notebook and pen from his pocket (a tape recorder being reserved for "formal statements") and began. "What time did you find Mr. Wright?"

I waited for Mother to answer, as she usually did in any police questioning, but she remained strangely mute.

"About a quarter to nine," I said, adding, "fifteen minutes before the Stroll ended."

Tony looked at Mother, and she nodded.

He asked, "How did you happen to find him?"

Again, Mother deferred to me.

"Well, there's not much to tell," I said. "Mother and I went to Simon's display, just to say hello, and when Simon wasn't there, we looked in the shed to see if he was inside. That's when . . . where . . . we found him."

"Did you see Mr. Wright any time prior to that?"

"Yes," I said. "But not to speak to him—more just to wave hello. He was already dealing with a long line of children."

"When was that?"

"When we first arrived at the Stroll, oh, about seven-thirty."

"Vivian? That right?"

Mother nodded.

Tony scribbled in the notebook.

He had a few more questions—had we noticed anyone loitering around Simon's display on either occasion we'd seen him? Did we have any idea how much money might have been in the donation bag?

To which we both answered, "No." Well, I answered "no" and Mother just shook her head.

Tony pocketed the notebook and pen, let out a sigh, and said, "That's all for now. I'll let you girls know if I need formal statements."

Mother stood. "Well, if there's nothing more, I'd like to retire. The Stroll left me quite exhausted."

"Certainly, Vivian," he said.

As Mother headed upstairs, I saw Tony to the front door. He was frowning.

He asked, "Where's the Vivian who tells me how to go about my job?"

"She and Simon were . . . good friends."

"So she's taking his death hard, then."

"I think maybe she is."

"Does that mean she'll stay out of this, and let the professionals handle the investigation without her 'help'?"

"Maybe." *Not a chance.*

He put an unprofessional and very gentle hand on my cheek. "And how about you, Brandy? Are you okay?"

"I'm fine."

Actually, I wasn't. But for once I wanted Tony to leave. I wanted to check on Mother, who really did seem to have been hit hard by Simon's murder.

He gave me a sweet peck of a kiss, then slipped out, and I had no sooner closed the door than Mother materialized at my side, like a jump cut in a film.

"Is he gone?"

"Yes."

"I thought he'd never leave!" she said, suddenly chipper. "Now, let's put our heads together about this new case! I'll get the incident board. . . ."

I smirked to myself—so she'd only been playing possum. Should have known.

"Mother, it's late," I said with a head shake and a sigh. "I really am exhausted, even if you aren't. Let's talk in the morning."

She tilted her head and narrowed her eyes in what might have been genuine concern. "You *do* look tired, dear. Very well, this can wait till breakfast."

A short time later, I lay in bed, Sushi curled near my feet. But sleep was a long time coming.

As it was for Mother . . . who I could hear crying softly in her room nearby.

Around eight the next morning, Sunday, Mother and I were seated at the antique Duncan Phyfe table in our Mediterranean-style dining room, about to have coffee and bagels, when the landline phone rang. I thought momentarily that it might be Tony, wanting us to come down for formal statements, but on reflection realized he would have more likely called my cell.

"Borne residence."

"Is this Vivian?" asked a woman's voice.

"No, it's her daughter—Brandy."

"Oh . . . well, I guess you'll do."

"Pardon?"

"This is Mildred Harper. Could you and your mother come over to my house right away? Is that possible?"

"I don't know. What's this about?"

"I'd rather tell you when you get here."

"Frankly, you're being awfully vague, and I'm afraid it's a little early for us."

There was a pause. "Well—is it too *early* for the Bornes to learn why Simon Wright was killed?"

"Meaning no offense, but the Bornes already know. Simon was killed for that missing donation money. A few measly dollars, a lot of it in change."

A brittle laugh. "You're closer than you think, when you say that. But you're still wrong, Ms. Borne. So very wrong. Would you like to get it right? For Mr. Wright?"

Thirty minutes later, Mother and I arrived at Mrs. Harper's house, one of a row of look-alike bungalows in a middle-income area of town.

According to Mother—who either knew or knew of just about everybody in town—Mrs. Harper was around seventy and a recent widow. She had one child, a son in his late forties named David, who was "a known slacker" (as Mother put it).

After greeting us at her door, Mrs. Harper—a plump diminutive woman wearing comfy pink sweats, her gray hair short and permed—escorted us into a small living room cluttered with bric-a-brac and furnished with the best Sears had to offer, twenty or thirty years ago.

As we settled on a gold corduroy couch, Mother asked, "Now, Mildred dear, what's this all about?"

Mildred, perching on the edge of a green faux-velvet recliner, replied, "When I heard that you were the ones who found poor Simon, I wanted to tell you something *before* I shared it with the authorities."

Mother straightened, a gleam coming to her slightly magnified eyes. Her mourning period had morphed into full investigative mode now, and how she *loved* to get out in front of the police.

"Very wise, dear," Mother said, nodding. "While they aren't completely incompetent, the Serenity P.D. haven't the track record in solving murders that my daughter and I have accumulated."

Mildred was smiling. "Yes, I've followed your exploits in the local paper, and in two or three of your books. That is exactly why I called you first. Also, Vivian, I, uh . . . I know that you and Simon were, at one time, well . . ."

"Yes," Mother said, "we were."

Our hostess processed that, then went on: "Simon Wright wasn't killed for a few dollar bills, I can assure you—but there *was* a valuable *coin* in the donation bag."

I sat forward. "And you know this how?"

"Because," she said, "I put it there."

Mother and I exchanged glances. Maybe this really was a murder case, not just a robbery gone awry.

"How valuable, Mildred?" Mother asked.

"About two hundred thousand dollars' worth."

Mother's mouth dropped open. Mine already had.

"It was an 1895 O Morgan silver dollar," the woman continued in a matter-of-fact manner, "that belonged to my late husband, who got it from his father. We had no idea it was worth so much until it was appraised as part of Morty's estate. I suppose I could have sold it and benefitted, but I'm content to live here in the house where we spent our marriage."

I couldn't help blurting, "So you *gave* it away?"

"I did," Mildred said with conviction. "I wanted to help Simon achieve his dream—to build a new domestic violence center on the site of the old orphanage." She paused, then added dramatically, "You see, I resided at the Serenity Home for Children once upon a time myself."

"I never knew that about you," Mother said, surprised.

Vivian Borne's knowledge of the denizens of Serenity and their personal histories apparently wasn't entirely complete after all.

Mildred was saying, "You'd be surprised who *did* reside there. Back then, such information was kept secret. Often the very young didn't even know they *were* an orphan unless the adoptive parents told them . . . and many thought it best not to."

"That's not common thinking now," I said.

"No, perhaps not. But it was a different time back then." Her gaze drifted up over our heads as she began to reminisce. "There were nearly two hundred of us when I was there, the home drawing from all around the state. And we weren't all orphans. If a single parent couldn't take care of their children, as was common in postwar years, the kids ended up with us. But we all got along and looked out for each other."

Her gaze went to Mother. "Simon Wright was like a big brother to me."

Mother asked, "*Simon* was an orphan, too?"

Mildred nodded. "And I can't help but feeling that . . . well, when Simon purchased the abandoned home and its grounds some years ago, he had a second purpose in mind: to make something *good* come of that place."

Mother was nodding, clearly following this. But I was in the dark.

"What do you mean?" I asked our hostess.

But it was Mother who answered: "Dear, there were certain . . . improprieties that came to light."

Mildred laughed once, humorlessly. "That's a mild way of putting it . . . abuse is more like it, and it didn't *all* come to light."

Mother raised a cautionary finger. "As I understand it, nothing was proved."

"The timing didn't allow it," Mildred countered. "By then, the government had instituted the foster care program and the orphanage was closed, taking many of its secrets with it."

I asked, "Did you witness any of this abuse?"

The woman shifted on the recliner. "Not exactly . . . I was fairly young, and wasn't there all that long before my adoptive parents took me home with them—but I *heard* things."

Had her imagination built those things into something even worse, I wondered?

I got the conversation back on point. "Mrs. Harper, who knew you were donating the coin?"

"No one."

"What about your son, David?" Mother asked. "Did you tell him of your intentions? And am I right in assuming your estate would otherwise be . . . modest?"

Her voice became defensive. "Yes, I'm not rich, we're not rich, but if you think David had anything to do with Simon's murder, you're wrong. My son may not be perfect, but he would never, *could* never do such a terrible thing!"

After assuring Mildred that we would do whatever we could to find Simon's killer, and her missing coin, Mother and I took our leave.

As we walked to the car, I asked, "Well, what do you think?"

"I think we should talk to less-than-perfect David. Don't you?"

I nodded. "I sure do. Someday *he'll* be an orphan, who might just prefer to inherit that coin himself."

Chapter Three

"Give her a dolly that laughs and cries
one that will open and shut her eyes . . ."

On the way to Happy Trails Trailer Court—where David Harper lived with a second wife half his age (both his marriages childless)—Mother said, "Mildred's imperfect boy has run afoul of the law several times."

"In what way?"

Mother raised an eyebrow. "Code ten and fifty-five."

She had a scanner in the kitchen and knew all the codes.

"Civilian translation please?" I requested.

"Civil fight in progress, and drunk driving."

Taking my eyes off the road momentarily, I said, "So little David has a temper. Either of those charges stick?"

"No. Mildred's impassioned pleading for her son had weight with the judge on both accounts, and he got off with fines . . . which *she* paid, I might add. Oh, and of course he lost his license for a time. That's what happens to people who aren't responsible behind the wheel."

At that I almost drove our car off the road myself, and if I *had* been drinking and driving (soft drink or coffee only), I'd have done a spit take. Mother's driver's license had been taken away from her numerous times, most recently for hit-and-run (knocking over a mailbox).

I pulled the car into the gravel entry of the trailer court and Mother directed me to Harper's mobile home, an older model with white siding stained by years of neglect, squatting on a tiny lot.

We got out of our car and approached the somewhat ominous trailer. Mother took the lead, going fearlessly up the three metal stairs, then knocking on a flimsy screen door.

She had not shared with me how she intended to approach David Harper, and I'd given her no suggestions, having no idea myself. Other than: *Hi! Your mother says you're too nice to kill Santa Claus for a valuable coin—is she right?*

A second knock summoned a skinny young woman with stringy brown hair and dull eyes, her jeans tight and torn and suited to her faded Harley Davidson T-shirt. Her thin arms were covered with tats, as if the shirt had colorful, tasteless sleeves.

"We don't take no salutation," she said. Her voice was a hospital-room flatline.

Mother smiled pleasantly. "My dear, we aren't *soliciting* anything, nor are we affiliated with any spiritual convocation hoping to bring you into the fold."

The tattooed woman blinked.

I discreetly kicked Mother's heel. "What she means is," I said, leaning around, "we're not selling anything or trying to get you to join our church."

"Oh. Then what *do* you want?"

Yes, excellent question—what *did* we want?

Mother cleared her throat and tried again. "Well, my dear, it seems our car has broken down and both our cell phones have died, and we wondered if you might let us use *your* phone to call a tow truck."

The young woman shrugged. "Sure, why not? I had cars break down on me plenty of times."

But then she pulled a phone out of a back pocket and handed it to Mother.

Mother took the cell, saying, "Why, thank you, dear, that's so very gracious of you . . ."

Think of all the trouble that could have been avoided in *Rocky Horror Picture Show* if Riff Raff had just offered Brad and Janet the use of a cell phone at the spooky mansion's front door.

Mother was vamping: ". . . but do you mind if I step inside? My poor old fingers are half-frozen."

The woman shrugged again. "Sure. It is frickin' cold."

Only she didn't say "frickin'."

Mother drawled (and here's where I should have kicked her again) in a stage Southern accent, "Why, thank you, young lady. I've always depended on the kindness of strangers."

To which she got, "Whatever."

The interior of the double-wide trailer was arrayed with furnishings that were surprisingly new—leather couch and matching recliner, glass coffee and end tables. Had she and David come into some money? Maybe enough to walk into a furniture showroom and say, "Wrap it up"?

Too soon for the coin to be fenced and sold, though; but maybe David had inherited *something* from his late father.

While Mother plopped down in an overstuffed chair, and began tapping numbers into the phone, I said, "I'm Brandy, and this is my mother, Vivian."

"Crystal."

Mother was speaking a little too loudly, overplaying her part. That's the problem with stage actresses in real life. "Hank's Towing Service? Yes . . . all right, yes of *course* I'll hold."

Since I knew of no such towing service, I wondered what confused soul had found himself or herself on the other end of that call. Surely no one named Hank.

With a nervous smile, I asked Crystal, "Did you go to the Holiday Stroll last night?"

"Nope."

"Did your husband go?"

Her eyes narrowed. "How'd you know I was married?"

I gestured to a framed, somewhat blurry wedding photo on an end table where the happy couple smiled for the camera. Crystal's wedding gown had long sleeves, so at least the tats weren't showing.

"Naw," she said, "Davey didn't go neither—that Christmas crap's a buncha bull. Anyway, Saturday night's his poker game."

I cocked my head and lowered my voice. "Did you hear about what happened?"

"Huh?"

"There was a murder there."

She reached for a pack of cigarettes on the nearby coffee table, extracted one and lit it, shrugging.

"Never heard about nothin' like that . . . Dave maybe did, but he never said nothin' to me about it." She blew smoke out the side of her mouth away from me, courteous hostess that she was. "Who bought it?"

"An older gentleman named Simon Wright. He was playing Santa Claus. He's done that for a lot of years."

She shrugged again. "Well, I didn't grow up around here. Never heard of him. Why'd somebody kill the guy, anyway?"

"Apparently for donation money he kept in a bag. Or maybe something else in that bag."

"Yeah?"

"Rumor is, there was something quite valuable in it."

There was a flicker in the young woman's dull eyes that quickly vanished, and she stubbed out the cigarette in an overflowing ashtray on an end table.

Mother said, "My apologies, kind lady . . . still holding!"

The door of the trailer opened and a tall, slender, hawkish-faced man in a hunting jacket, jeans, and heavy boots burst in.

He saw Mother and me and growled, "What are these two snoops doing here?"

"Their car broke down," Crystal said.

"My behind!" David snapped. Only he didn't say "behind." "Don't you know who they are, you idiot?"

His helpmate shook her head.

He whipped an accusing finger at each of us. "These are the two local screwballs who go around sticking their nose in everybody else's business!"

Hard to argue with that. . . .

"Hey!" Crystal blurted. "Don't get mad at *me* about it! I don't know them from an atom. I ain't from around here, remember."

David now turned his red-faced fury on us. It was like an oven door opened suddenly, minus any enticing food smells. "Have you been talking to my mother? About that damn coin?"

Mother stood. "Yes."

He took a few steps toward her, and I moved to block him.

"She called *us,*" I told him. "Said she had gone to the Stroll last night and put that coin in Simon Wright's donation bag. You *do* know that he was killed, and the money in the bag was stolen?"

"You think I live under a rock or something?"

Mother said, "I assume that's a rhetorical question."

David smirked at us. "I suppose you two female clowns think *I* did it?"

Mother asked, "We think you're innocent until proven guilty. But we can start with, this poker game you attended last night—could you provide the names of the other players?"

He thrust a finger at the door. "We can *start* with get the fudge out . . . the both of you!" Only he didn't say . . . you know.

Mother handed Crystal back the cell phone. "Thank you, dear, you've been so kind."

"But what about the tow truck?" she asked.

David rolled his eyes and said, "There's no tow truck, you dumb ditz."

Crystal said, "There is so! I heard her call one."

And not wanting to add any further sour notes to such marital harmony, Mother and I beat a hasty retreat.

Our next stop was to pay a visit to Simon Wright's daughter and son-in-law, Della and Rod Conklin, ostensibly to offer our sympathy.

Mother filled me in on the way.

"Della was an only child," Mother said, adding, "spoiled rotten, I'm afraid. And when she married Rod, it broke Simon's heart."

"Why?"

She shook her head, frowning. "He never said exactly why. But I think we can safely assume that Simon must have known about the man's abusive behavior. I myself heard several code ten-sixteens that brought police to their door."

"Why do you suppose Della put up with that?"

Mother sighed. "There are many reasons why someone stays in an abusive relationship . . . fear, shame, the belief that the person is going to change, even that the beating was somehow deserved. Anyway, while I don't know the details, Simon made it clear to me that Della's refusal to leave Rod caused a rupture in the father/daughter relationship."

I nodded. "That might be another reason for Simon's interest in funding a new domestic violence center."

I steered the car onto Shady Lane, which cut through a middle-class housing addition built in the 1960s. We parked in front of a modest one-story ranch-style home, got out, and made our way to the door. I was still content to let Mother lead the way.

Rod Conklin, wearing a green rugby shirt and jeans, answered the door. In his forties, Della's husband was well under six feet but sturdy-looking, with short brown hair, a crooked nose, and a slash for a mouth.

"Oh," he said flatly, eyes narrowing. There was something at least vaguely accusatory when he said: "You're the ones that found Simon. Vivian and . . . ?"

"Brandy. Borne."

He nodded. His expression remained blank and yet I sensed suspicion. "Is there something I do for you?"

Clasping her hands to her bosom, Mother said, "We came to offer Della our condolences. I was a good friend of her father's."

He frowned. "Well, uh . . . she really doesn't want to see anybody just now."

Why? I thought. *A black eye she's nursing, maybe?*

"Let them in," a female voice behind Rod said.

Rod stepped aside and we entered a small foyer. The voice belonged to Della, whose idea of mourning was a white sweater and black slacks. Simon's daughter was about as tall as her husband, with chin-length hair a shade of red unknown in nature, her face a feminine softening of her father's features.

She stood at the mouth of the living room and gestured for us to follow her. The room was tastefully decorated in pastel shades, with Christmas touches here and there: a tree festooned with ornaments; a collection of wooden nutcracker figures; a grouping of ceramic angels.

Mother said, "My dear, how are you holding up?"

Della's eyes were neither swollen nor runny-mascara black. Nor were they red from crying.

There was no offer for us to sit.

"I'm fine, thank you," Della replied, something cold about it. "Since you and my father were close, I'm sure you know he and I hadn't gotten along for some time."

"Yes, of course," Mother replied, retaining a sympathetic tone. "But that doesn't make a tragedy like this any easier—in fact, it can make it even harder."

Rod, on the periphery, addressed his wife: "Darling—could I get you and our guests anything to drink?"

How typical of his type to put on a good show in front of company.

Della said brusquely, "I don't believe they'll be staying that long."

Surprised by her rudeness (never mind that we were there on false pretenses), I said, "I don't mean to sound cruel, Mrs. Conklin—but don't you *care* who killed your father?"

Della's expression changed, the words making some impact. "Actually . . . I do care. *Of course* I care. I obviously want my father's murderer to be caught, whoever he might be."

Or she.

Mother moved in. "We're conducting an unofficial investigation of sorts. Perhaps you're aware of the successes my daughter and I have had in aiding the local constabulary."

Della nodded, shrugged.

"Then," Mother went on with a pleasant smile, "I'm sure you won't mind answering a few questions . . ."

"I suppose not."

"Did you or your husband, together or separately, attend the Stroll last night?"

Simultaneously Della said yes and Rod replied no.

Mother asked, "Which is it?"

Della said, "We *were* downtown, both of us, early on . . . but when the Stroll really got under way, started really getting crowded, we left and came home."

I asked, "While you were there, did you see Simon?"

The pair shook their heads, Della adding, "Only from a distance . . . As I say, we had no real contact with him for years."

Rod said, "The police told us Simon was robbed, the donation bag emptied, and that's likely why . . . why this awful thing happened." He shook his head. "Whoever did it couldn't have got much for his trouble."

Or hers.

Mother then told the couple about the valuable coin donated by Mildred Harper, news that seemed to surprise them.

Della said, "Then my father's death wasn't so senseless."

That struck me as odd, as if she were somehow condoning the killing.

Mother, apparently feeling that she'd gotten all the information she could, said, "Well, we've taken up enough of your time. Thank you for putting up with us at a moment like this."

We said our good-byes, which were perfunctory and quick.

Back home in our library room, Mother wheeled out from behind the stand-up piano the old schoolroom blackboard that she used to compile her suspect lists.

While I sat on the piano bench, she picked up a piece of white chalk from the board's lip and wrote:

VICTIM: SIMON WRIGHT

Suspect	Opportunity	Motive
David Harper	poker game (TBC)*	valuable coin
Rod Conklin	yes	wife's inheritance

Potential Accessory
Crystal Harper
Della Conklin

*To Be Confirmed

"Not much to go on," I said.

"I concur," Mother sighed. She had a sheet of paper and was taping it on the side of the blackboard.

I got up for a look, and my mouth dropped open. "Where did you get *that*?"

It was a printout photo of the crime scene.

Mother shrugged. "I took it with my cell phone while you were outside waiting for the police to arrive."

I didn't know whether to chastise her for a lack of common decency or congratulate her for her dogged resourcefulness. I did neither, because I noticed something in the photo that sent me rushing off.

A few minutes later, I came back with a copy of the photo *I* had taken that night of Simon and his display.

Taping my printout next to Mother's, I asked, "Notice anything different about Simon's suit in the photos?"

She said, "Well, let me see . . . you know, I *always* find the differences in the Hocus Focus feature in the comic section."

Mother leaned in for a closer look, big eyes behind the large glasses going back and forth as if she were watching a tennis match.

"I've got it!" she said gleefully.

"Do you?"

"Indeed. The sleeve and trouser cuffs in your photo don't have any fur! That means there were two *different* Santa suits worn that night."

"The significance of which is . . . ?"

"Simon must have been murdered at the beginning of the Stroll, not at the end. The killer in the furless cuffs had taken his place!"

"Which means something else, too."

"What, dear?"

"Simple. Simon wasn't giving you the cold shoulder after all."

Mother nodded, her eyes welling with tears. "Because Simon wasn't really . . . Simon."

Chapter Four

"Ho, ho, ho! Who wouldn't know?
Ho, ho, ho! Who wouldn't know?"

Dearest ones!

This is Vivian, a.k.a. Mother, taking the narrative reins from dear Brandy to give you a fresh perspective. But before I continue, there are a few issues I simply must address.

Firstly, some readers reported that they had become quite ill in the aftermath of making (and apparently eating the results of) the recipe for Iowa State Fair Fried Butter that we included in *Antiques Swap.* Might I remind those afflicted readers that we also included an extensive food warning. (If you must blame someone, however, blame Brandy, since including the recipe was her idea.) (In her slight defense, I should add that Brandy reported her own unfortunate abdominal distress after eating this deep-fried delicacy.)

Secondly—and please note that I use the preferred form of enumeration (according to Wiktionary) rather than "first," followed by "second"—shoot. I forgot what I was secondly going to say.

Oh! Several readers expressed their disappointment that in *Antiques Slay Ride* I failed to regale them with one of my usual witty tales about the passengers I encounter on the trolley. *Mea culpa!* Here, by way of making amends, is a doozy. (Hope I'm not making a tactical error by building it up too much.)

Anywho, one Christmastime several years past, I had hitched a ride on the gas-converted trolley, which provides free rides to Serenity shoppers heading downtown to spend their hard-earned (not filthy) lucre. The trolley was crowded that afternoon, but a few seats remained, so no one had to give theirs up when Billy Buckly hopped aboard.

Billy was a little person (the PC term for "dwarf" or "midget") whose grandfather appeared in the 1939 film *The Wizard of Oz* as one of the Munchkin midgets (here the term seems permissible because firstly, the term at the time wasn't negative, and secondly, Billy's gramps was one of the Singer Midgets, a performing group). So here the term is "grandfathered in," so to speak.

If you'll excuse me a moment, I think perhaps I've neglected to take my daily dosage of bipolar medication . . .

. . . and I'm back!

Returning to our delightful anecdote, Billy was dressed as an elf (that's not un-PC, is it?) and he was on his way to Ingram's Department Store to appear in support of their Santa. Billy headed down the trolley aisle, handing out candy canes to each and every one, then settled into a vacant seat, disappearing behind the seat back in front of him.

At the next stop, the widow Althrop got on, a rather plump individual perhaps too fond of her own German cooking, and took the last remaining seat, which happened to be in front of the diminutive star of our story. Apparently, the widow Althrop hadn't seen Billy, because when he popped up in his elf outfit (perhaps I failed to mention that his face was painted green) to tap her on the shoulder and offer her a candy cane, she turned, stood, and let out a scream that so startled the driver, he slammed on the brakes and little Billy would have gone flying straight into dire circumstances if it hadn't been for Mrs. Althrop's ample bosom. Well, wouldn't you know it, but the very next week they were dating!

Monday morning—with our antiques store closed (open Tuesday through Saturday) and Brandy there putting out Christmas merchandise—I was free to do some quality investigating on my own.

Due to a handful of vehicular infractions of which I'd been wrongly accused (sometimes the System just doesn't work!), the trolley was my preferred mode of transportation whenever

Brandy was unavailable (or unwilling) to chauffeur me around.

The trolley left me off in front of Hunter's Hardware Store, a uniquely Midwestern aberration: while the front section of the elongated emporium sold everything one might expect of a modern (modernish) hardware business, the rear was given over to a small bar, offering hard liquor to hard workers who came in for hardware. Hardly a desirable combo, this cocktail of liquor libations and power tools, several inebriated customers having staggered home with a brand-new electrical implement only to saw off a finger, nail a foot to the floor, or (to cite a recent example) drill a hole through a previously perfect hand.

That was the price of getting hammered at Hunter's Hardware.

Mary and Junior were the proprietors, Mary running the cash register, Junior pouring the drinks. The middle-aged couple bought the business some years ago with the money Junior's better half received after losing a leg in a freak accident while on vacation in Los Angeles. (I can't elaborate any more about said accident since receiving a *second* cease-and-desist letter warning that I am not even to *hint* at what attraction it was—and certainly I was not about to imply that the accident had anything to do with a very large mechanical ocean mammal with extremely sharp teeth.)

Mary—who might be best if impolitely described as "dumpy" (though I'd never do such a thing), her brownish gray hair worn in a tight bun—was occupied with a customer. I just breezed on by with a polite wave and headed to the back bar, where Junior—a paunchy, mottled-nosed sort who perhaps liked to sample his own merchandise a tad too much (and I'm not talking about hammers and screwdrivers) (maybe screwdrivers)—was busy polishing tumblers.

Well, "busy" might be overstating it.

I slid up onto a burst-leather stool in front of him.

"Your usual, Vivian?" he asked pleasantly.

He meant a Shirley Temple (may she rest in peace). I'd learned long ago not to mix alcohol with my medication—you would, too, if you wound up in Kalamazoo with no idea how you got there.

"Please, kind sir."

Junior turned his back for just under a minute, then placed the sweet concoction on the bar as if presenting a prize.

"Terrible shame about Simon," he said, and gave his big head a glum shake. "Heard you and Brandy found 'im. You're kind of gettin' a knack for that sort of thing."

I took a dainty sip. "That's right," I told him ambiguously. My visit was not to engage Junior—who usually added little to my investigations, thanks to his ever-dwindling supply of brain cells—but rather to wring some facts out of Henry, like one of Junior's bar rags.

Seated several stools down, Henry was Hunter's perennial barfly, a formerly prominent surgeon who had once taken a shot of whiskey to steady his hands, then removed a patient's appendix instead of his gallbladder, effectively ending his career (the surgeon's, not the patient's).

Henry was a bony senior citizen with silver hair, a beaky nose, and his original teeth. He had been off the sauce for a good while, thanks to Junior and me coming up with a scheme: Junior offered him free beer, and then (unbeknownst to Henry) served him only alcohol-free product. And Henry could whip up a placebo-effect drunk that rivaled the real thing.

But as I collected my Shirley Temple and moved down to talk to Henry, I became alarmed by what appeared to be a tumbler of whisky before him, instead of a glass of near beer.

"Hello, Henry," I said, putting one stool between us.

"'Lo, Viv," he slurred.

I shot Junior an accusatory look, and he gave me an apologetic shrug, mouthing the word "Simon."

So, the death of Serenity's Santa Claus had caused Henry to demand the hard stuff. And, having been unknowingly off the real thing for months, Henry was now drunker than a skunk without half trying. (Are skunks really known to seek out alcoholic refreshment? It would seem unlikely in the wild.)

Luckily, Henry's brain cells seemed to work fine both on and off the sauce; he was just easier to understand, ersatz blasted.

I said, "I know you and Simon were pals, Henry, and I'm sorry for your loss." Simon had never abandoned the surgeon-turned-town-drunk when so many others had.

Henry nodded, staring into his drink.

I went on: "So I just *know* you'll want to do everything you can to help me catch his killer."

"Shuh-shuh-should of 'ported it," he mumbled.

My ears perked, much as Sushi's do when I open a bag of corn curls (puff not crispy).

"Reported what?" I asked.

He seemed about to nod off, so I prodded, "Henry! Is it something to do with Simon's murder?"

Henry shook his head. "Not 'im . . . 'er."

"Her? Her who?"

"Nersh." Henry shook his head sorrowfully. "Shuh-uh . . . should've . . . but din."

"Didn't what, dear?"

"Din do anythin'."

"When was this?"

"Long time, long, long time . . ."

And that was the last I got from Henry.

I picked up Shirley and moved back down to Junior, reclaiming my former stool.

"You need to get him back on the O'Doul's," I whispered, "pronto."

"Don't I know it," Junior sighed, putting down his bar towel. "Came in this morning demandin' whiskey, and I couldn't talk him out of it. Been like that for hours."

"Would you happen to know what he's talking about?"

Junior shrugged. "I think he was sayin' 'nurse.' Maybe somebody he worked with, at the hospital, 'fore he lost his license? I didn't get a name."

Out of the corner of my eye, I'd been watching Mary hobble over from the cash register with her ill-fitting prosthetic leg. Arriving, she lit into her husband, "If you don't find that Santa suit, Junior Hunter, I'm takin' it out of your till!"

"What Santa suit?" I asked calmly, though within me excitement spiked.

She swivelled to me, her leg squeaking like a rusty gate. "The one Junior rented to wear during the Stroll! I told him it was inappropriate, a Santa Claus bartender."

Junior said, "So I just hung it behind the bar—and somebody musta swiped it. You *believe* people these days?"

I asked, "Who was in the bar that night, Junior?"

"All kinds of folks."

"Let's limit it to men—*before* the Stroll started."

Junior frowned in thought. "Jeez, Viv, I was awful busy. . . ."

Busy sampling the sauce, no doubt.

"But," he continued, "a few of the Romeos stopped in, and were camped out at a table. They might have some idea who was in here."

This being Monday, I knew just where to find the Romeos (Retired Old Men Eating Out)—they'd be having an early lunch at Boonie's, a recently opened upscale sports bar downtown.

I hoofed it over to Iowa Avenue where the restaurant took up the first floor of a beautifully restored Victorian edifice. The interior, however, had been completely remodeled with nothing dating back but for the original redbrick walls. Now it was all modern tables and chairs, colorful sports memorabilia, and endless huge flat-screen TVs displaying a dizzying variety of sports channels. The sound was turned down on them all in favor of Bing Crosby, Frank Sinatra, and Andy Williams doing seasonal favorites. Right now soccer fans were screaming silently and Bing was singing "Silent Night" loudly.

At a little after eleven, only a few patrons were on hand, and I easily spotted the Romeos seated at a rectangular table for six, having platters of juicy burgers and crispy fries. They really shouldn't be eating such fare, what with their various health issues (too numerous to mention), but I would let that pass for the present. I had bigger burgers to fry.

Today, only four Romeos were present, thanks to colds and flu making the winter rounds, not to mention the Grim Reaper occasionally dropping by. Present and accounted for were Harold, ex-army sergeant; Vern, retired chiropractor; Randall, former hog farmer; and Christopher, chairman of the board of the First National Bank. Chris was only semiretired, but the group let him in because the banker knew all the inside dope among Serenity's highest social circles.

The Romeos had recently joined a fantasy football league and, reading their dour expressions, I deduced that over the weekend their fantasy team must have done poorly in its fantasy game, perhaps racking up a low fantasy score. (FYI: None of the Romeos was my fantasy.)

Nonetheless, I purred in my best Edie Adams doing Mae West manner, "Hello, *boys*—mind if I join you?"

Normally, the female of the species was not welcome at a Romeo table, but I was the exception, the eternal Shirley MacLaine of their geriatric Rat Pack.

My greeting resulted in an affirmative reaction and I plopped down in a chair next to Vern. Harold sat across from me with Randall to his left. Chris was at one end of the table as if conducting a board meeting.

Harold said, "Heard you and Brandy discovered poor Simon." The ex-army sergeant, who looked something like Bob Hope (the older Bob Hope), shook his head. "Awful, just awful."

"Awful indeed," I replied. What good did saying it was awful do? Finding the killer was the only way to do anything about it.

A waitress wearing embellished jeans and a black T-shirt that read BE NICE OR LEAVE appeared at my side and asked, "Anything today, hon?"

"Just black coffee, please."

When she'd gone, I turned to Chris. "Since your bank has been sponsoring Simon's Santa display all these years, am I correct in assuming he had his donation account with you?"

Chris nodded. The banker reminded me vaguely of Ricardo Montalbán (without the accent): *Fantasy Island*, from a distance; *Star Trek II: The Wrath of Khan*, up close. He was the only one of the four in a real suit, not a jogging outfit.

"So what will happen to the money?" I asked him. "I know Simon intended it to go to the building of a new domestic violence shelter on the old orphanage grounds."

"If you mean, can his daughter get her hands

on it?" he replied. "Thankfully, no. The beneficiary on the account is the current shelter."

Which shared the old YMCA building downtown with the homeless.

"If you don't mind my asking," I said, "how much is in the account?"

His smile was patronizing. "Vivian, I don't mind you asking. But you must know I can't tell you."

I shrugged. "Can't blame a girl for trying."

Vern, the retired chiropractor who'd have made a decent stand-in for the older Clark Gable, said, "Not to tell tales out of school, but Simon told me last year he'd collected about a hundred grand so far."

Randall, former pig farmer, a less (much less) sophisticated Sydney Greenstreet, added, "Last I heard, it was up to one hundred twenty-five. And Simon already owned the land."

Chris said, "Which the *shelter* will own, after the estate is probated."

Harold said, "Still . . . it's far short of the three hundred grand or so Simon said he needed for the new center."

My coffee had arrived and I took a dainty sip before dropping the bomb.

"Mildred Harper," I said, "put a silver coin worth two hundred thousand dollars in Simon's donation bag the night of the Stroll. *That* would have put the project over the top."

Such revelations are, dear reader, why the old gents invariably welcome me to their table. That and my feminine wiles.

This particular revelation earned me audible gasps—punctuated by a few clacking dentures.

Chris, wide-eyed, asked, "Are you *sure* about that?"

I gave *him* a patronizing smile. "I heard it directly from Mildred herself."

The banker asked, "Just what kind of coin was it?"

I made them all wait while I had another sip. Darned good coffee!

Then I said, "An 1895 O Morgan silver dollar."

Chris sat back. "Good Lord . . . that *is* rare. I've only heard of one other turning up in my entire banking career."

Randall was going, "Ooooh ooooh," Gunther Toody-style. (For you youngsters, refer to Google—search *Car 54, Where Are You?*)

All eyes went to the former pig farmer, who proclaimed, "I bet Mildred's *son* killed Simon—*what's* that no-good's name?"

"David," Vern said. "Definitely on the naughty-not-nice list, that one."

Harold snapped his fingers. "That lowlife was hanging around at Hunter's the night of the Stroll—when the four of us stopped in for a beer, remember, men? Grousing about some *coin* he thought he deserved . . . I guess now we know *what* coin."

So much for poker with the boys.

"You know who *else* was there?" Chris chimed in. "Simon's daughter and son-in-law!" The others nodded, remembering. "And they could have easily overheard David. . . ."

Harold said skeptically, "Come on, Chris. Sure, they were estranged and all, but Della wouldn't kill her own father."

"Who says?" Vern said with a skeptical head shake. "She's got one nasty temper—look how she beats up on that poor husband of hers!"

And such revelations were why *I* sought out a seat at the Romeos' table.

"What's that?" I asked, not sure I heard correctly (pesky earwax buildup).

"Never knew that, Viv?" the retired chiropractor asked. "You disappoint me. Of course, I used to *work* on Rod. He'd come in with a dislocated shoulder or whatever, and have some excuse for the injury . . . but the bruises told another story."

I'd assumed the code 16s had meant a husband hitting his wife, not the other way around.

I asked, "Did any of you gents happen to notice a Santa suit hanging behind the bar at Hunter's last night?"

In return for this seeming non sequitur, the men gave me puzzled looks.

"What gives, Viv?" Harold asked.

"Junior's Santa suit went missing—this was shortly before the start of the Stroll when Simon was killed."

Randall raised a correcting finger. "You mean, at the *end* of the Stroll."

"No," I said. "Simon was killed *before* it began. Whoever murdered him stole Junior's Santa suit, then impersonated Simon for the rest of the event . . . with Simon dead in the woodshed behind him, and an upset reindeer next to him."

Chris was shaking his head. "That's impossible,

Vivian. I spoke to Simon around eight-thirty, half an hour before the Stroll ended."

I arched an eyebrow. "Are you sure it was Simon?"

"Well, certainly!" the banker was quick to answer. But then he frowned. "I mean, I *think* it was Simon. Of course, he *was* wearing that heavy false beard and Santa cap. . . ."

"And you *expected* it to be him."

Chris nodded, adding, "Why wouldn't I?"

"What did you talk about?"

"I really don't recall . . . it was just a brief social conversation." He paused, adding, "Come to think of it, I did most of the talking."

The group fell silent for a moment, then Harold asked, as if to himself, "Why would someone impersonate Simon? It doesn't make sense."

"It does," I said, "*if* the killer wanted to confuse the time of death."

Vern asked, "Wouldn't the cold weather do that anyway?"

"Possibly," I answered. "But any pathologist worth his or her salt would take that into consideration."

I told them about Henry's strange babbling, a by-product of the poor man falling off the wagon.

"Simon's death must have really set him off," Randall offered.

Vern, to my left, twisted toward me. "You say Henry mentioned a *nurse*? Did he mention a name?"

I shook my head. "Only that he should have reported her—I assumed it was someone he worked with at the hospital, years ago."

Vern's expression turned troubled. "You know, when Henry was first practicing, he made regular visits to the orphanage to tend to the children—colds and childhood maladies, plus the kind of scrapes and injuries kids get playing. Henry could have been referring to the nurse there—Maude Tanner."

The name stirred a distant memory. "Wasn't she accused of physically disciplining the children, to the point of abuse? Whatever happened to her?"

Vern shrugged. "She *conveniently* left town before any charges were filed. And shortly after that? The orphanage closed down."

I turned toward him and narrowed my eyes. "You seem to know a lot about the woman, Vern."

He shrugged. "I should . . . I lived out there as a child."

I squinted at him. "Why was that?"

"Why do you think, Viv? Why does any kid live at an orphanage? I was an orphan."

"As was I," Randall said, nodding.

Harold shifted in his seat. "Me, too."

Chris held a hand up, palm out. "Not guilty." He laughed lightly. "But they let me join the group anyway."

Well, dear reader, I could have fallen out of my chair! The files at the orphanage had been well-sealed indeed, if Vivian Borne knew nothing of their contents. And now I understood that the bond the core group of Romeos shared was more than a love of fattening food.

My cell phone trilled—Brandy.

"Mother," she said, excitedly, "you're not going to *believe* what I'm about to tell you. . . ."

I listened, knowing that I might well have said the same thing to her.

Chapter Five

"Up on the housetop, click, click, click
Down through the chimney with
old Saint Nick . . ."

Brandy back.

It was nine by the time I rolled out of bed Monday morning and stumbled down to the kitchen to find a note from Mother by the coffee machine saying she had "errands to run."

Translation: She'd taken the trolley downtown to do some snooping.

A postscript said I'd find breakfast warming in the oven, which turned out to be one of my favorite Danish delights Mother makes around Christmastime.

Hof Pandekager
(Court Pancakes)

Filling:

3 egg yolks
¼ cup sugar
1 orange; juiced, peel grated
¼ cup butter

Batter:

¾ cup flour
½ tsp salt
1 tsp baking powder
2 tbsp powdered sugar
2 eggs
1 tsp cognac
⅔ whole milk
⅓ water (mixed with milk)

Make the filling first by beating the yolks and sugar together in the upper part of a double boiler until well mixed; add the grated orange peel and juice, mixing well; add butter in dabs or small pieces. Cook until thickened. Let cool.

To make the batter, sift flour, salt, baking powder, and powdered sugar together. In separate bowl, beat the eggs slightly and stir into flour mixture. Gradually add the cognac and milk/water, beating well. Let stand fifteen minutes. Bake cakes on well-buttered griddle, browning on both sides. Remove cakes from griddle and add a tablespoon of cooled filling to the center of each; roll the cake around the filling to make a sausage shape. Arrange on an oven-proof serving dish; sprinkle with extra powdered sugar; set dish under low broiler heat to lightly brown the tops. Makes sixteen small cakes, or eight large cakes.

I helped myself to two cakes, giving some morsels to Sushi by way of mixing them in with her dry dog food so that she'd eat all the food, and I could give her an insulin shot. Which she did and I did.

After my shower, I got into my favorite DKNY jeans and a Splendid plaid shirt. Today Sushi and I'd be going to the shop—even though it was closed—because I still had several boxes of Christmas merchandise to put out, and time was running short, only so many more shopping days and all that.

Downstairs I threw on my military-style coat, grabbed my purse (a black Hobo cross body), scooped up Sushi, and we headed out to the car.

Our shop was unique in that it took up an entire house—a two-story white clapboard built around the turn of last century and locally infamous as the site of two ax murders (see *Antiques Chop*), which is why we got the place so cheap.

Our antiques and collectibles were displayed in the proper room—that is, living-room furniture in the living room; kitchenware in the kitchen; books in the library; bedroom sets upstairs; linens in the closets. In the basement we'd recently added "Mantiques" (old tools, fishing gear, beer signs, pinup calendars, and so forth) to lure male customers or at least give the fellas something to do while the gals shopped upstairs. Everyone knew just where to go in the house to look for whatever they were after.

Anyway, at the shop, I dragged down several boxes from the attic (nothing up there but storage and cobwebs) containing a variety of holiday merchandise—vintage Christmas cards, glass ornaments, assorted plaster and plastic Santas, and so forth—that I planned on salting around the various rooms.

As Sushi looked on, I was sorting through the boxes in the ample entryway, in front of the checkout counter, when someone knocked on the locked front door.

I saw Tony through the top glass of the door and went to unlock it.

Serenity's top cop stomped the snow from his Florsheims and stepped in, his dark wool topcoat open over the usual blue shirt, navy tie, and gray slacks.

"What's so important that you had to see me now?" he asked, the slight irritation in his voice something only a girlfriend could detect.

On the drive to the shop I'd debated long and hard whether to show Tony the two pictures Mother and I had taken of Simon. My loyalty to Mother in keeping her investigation self-contained was becoming increasingly compromised by my desire to help Tony in his job.

"I would've come to the station," I said, "but they said you were out, so I sent you that text. . . ."

Crooking a finger for him to follow, I went over to where both photos lay on the counter.

When Tony saw Mother's crime-scene shot, his face turned a Christmassy red. "Where the hell d'you get that?"

This time you would not have to be his girlfriend to pick up on the irritation.

"Mother took it with her cell—you can deal with her later."

Tapping the other photo, I explained the difference in the suits, and the theory that Simon had actually been killed at the beginning of the Stroll.

Red fading, Tony nodded. "That makes sense. Indicates why our interviews with eye witnesses don't jibe with the preliminary autopsy report."

A little bell tinkled, telling me I'd forgotten to relock the front door, and someone came in—some customer I'd have to turn away.

Only it wasn't a customer—rather, it was Dumpster Dan, in the too-big tattered overcoat he'd worn at the Stroll, moving toward us, face flushed.

"I *know* you're closed," he apologized breathlessly, "but I saw the lights on and just couldn't wait."

The man's bloodshot eyes went to Tony. "And I'm glad *you're* here, too, Chief Cassato . . . because I want you to know that I found this in a Dumpster . . . and finders keepers, right?"

Dan held up a clenched fist.

Tony, who had a certain fondness for Dan,

said gently, "Well, that depends. Sometimes things get thrown away accidentally."

"Oh." Dan seemed to deflate.

"But if *that* is the case," Tony went on, "there might well be a reward."

"Oh!" Dan filled right back up.

I asked, "What do you have there, Dan? Something special?"

"I think so." He opened his palm, and the moment I saw the shiny silver object, I knew what it was.

So did Tony.

"Mind if I see that?" Tony asked evenly, so as not to spook the man.

Dan handed over the rare silver dollar.

Examining the coin, Tony asked, "Where did you find this?"

"In a Dumpster behind Hunter's."

"When?"

"This morning."

"Any more money? *Newer* money?"

Dan looked down at his feet.

"Dan," Tony said patiently, "any more money?"

"Well . . . there *were* some bills, small ones, and a buncha change, too—but I didn't have time to get much of it before the Dumpster truck rolled up. Guess I can't keep any of the money, huh?"

"Sorry, no," Tony said.

Dan sighed. "Afraid of that." A pause. "But is it okay if I keep that Santa suit?"

Actually, it wasn't.

And after Tony had left with Dan to take him to the station for further questioning, I called

Mother on her cell and told her what had just transpired.

After the expected gasp, she announced, "So! . . . Simon's death was *not* about someone stealing the coin for monetary gain!"

"Then what *was* it about?"

"That's what we're going to find out—come and get me at Boonie's. I think it's time we pay a visit to the old orphanage."

With Mother giving directions, Sushi in her lap listening intently, I drove out in the country 5.7 miles, then turned down a snowy narrow lane, coming to a stop in front of an austere, multi-gabled Gothic structure of red sandstone.

"The orphanage was once the manor of a wealthy pearl button manufacturer," Mother said, "himself an orphan who grew to success and wealth."

We were seated in the car, gazing out at the decaying edifice.

"And," Mother continued, "when the manufacturer died in the early 1920s, childless, a widower, he left the mansion to the county on the condition that it be used for an orphanage. Then, when it closed in the 1960s, Simon bought the property for a song. But our favorite Santa never developed it. He had long-term plans for the land."

"What about the coin? Why was it stolen only to be discarded?"

She stared at the old orphanage. "I believe it

may have been about stopping any construction on this site."

"Why?"

"Because, dear, new construction might turn up a very old body."

She told me about the notorious nurse, Maude Tanner.

"So we're here to find a body?" I asked, goggling at her. Every time I think I've heard her worst idea, she tops herself.

But Mother's only answer was to exit the car, and I hurried to catch up with her, setting Sushi down. We three went up the dozen or so crumbling cement steps to a wide porch precariously held up with rotting wooden columns.

Mother tried the heavy front door and found it locked.

Undaunted, she said, "There must be a key around here *somewhere.*"

"Under the welcome mat, maybe? Gee, for some reason there *isn't* a welcome mat here at Friday the Thirteenth Orphanage."

But Mother tried various possible hiding places anyway, and came up empty. I tried, too, with no better luck.

A familiar barking came from inside, and suddenly Sushi's furry face popped up between slats of a boarded-up porch window.

"Well, *she* got in," I said, amazed.

"Let's ask her how," Mother replied.

"Sushi's smart, Mother, but she doesn't talk."

"Her tracks in the snow do!"

We followed the little tracks around back

where the prints went up stone steps to a smaller porch, stopping beneath a boarded-up first-floor window. One board had fallen away, allowing room enough for doggie entry. But I easily removed another rotting board, allowing Mother and me to climb over the sill.

We found ourselves in a large kitchen, although few remnants remained to indicate that other than the linoleum-topped counters. The cupboards had been torn out, leaving ugly scars, light fixtures ripped from the ceiling, frayed electrical wires dangling like stripped veins.

Mother said, "Scavengers."

"Well, at least the stuff's being recycled."

"I'm glad to hear such a positive attitude coming from you, dear. Because we have things to do."

Sushi scampered to a stop at my feet. Feeling certain that she wouldn't wander too far, I let her roam free, confident she would only sniff and look into any holes in the floor, not fall in. I wished I was as confident about Mother and me.

We moved along a long dark hallway to the front of the building where the midafternoon sun coming through the space between the slats of boarded-up windows gave us some light, at least.

In the once-grand parlor, the scavengers had been even more bold, removing all the wainscoting from the lower sections of walls, leaving only faded floral wallpaper and the dirty outlines of where pictures had hung. A large fireplace had been robbed of its mantel.

The house was giving me the willies, even if I

wasn't sure what the willies were, and to compensate I joked, "Maybe our nurse got stuffed up the chimney."

Mother said, "I don't think so, dear. . . . I'm not getting any vibes."

She claimed to get such vibes when her bunions were hurting her, which was a psychic feat no matter how you spelled it.

Mother moved on to the dining room and I followed. Here most of the parquet floor had been hauled off, along with a hanging light fixture, leaving a good-sized hole in the middle of the ceiling.

We returned to the main hallway and climbed a wide, wooden staircase that, remarkably, still retained its oak banister—too big and awkward to haul away, maybe. As I went up, my hand slid along the smooth wood as hundreds of children's hands once had done.

The second floor had been made into one large, long room.

"This is where the girls slept," Mother said, giving me a guided tour I didn't remember requesting. "They each had their own bed."

Nearby a single twin-sized iron bed with rusty springs lay on its side, with a shredded mattress home to a nest of mice.

Even back then, this must have been a dreary place, and I tried to imagine what life must have been like for the children here, each one waiting and hoping to be adopted. Wind whispering through a cracked window seemed to say, *"Pick me, pick me."* You didn't have to believe in haunted houses to sense the ghosts in this ravaged structure.

Mother led our hunt for Nurse Tanner onward, up a narrow creaking staircase to the attic.

Continuing with the tour, Mother said, "And this is where the boys were housed."

She said that as if the boys were things not humans, but there was no question they'd had it tougher than the girls: sleeping with open ceiling beams, rough wood floor, and few windows for light.

Sushi sneezed from the dust.

I trailed Mother over to a vertical support beam where boys had crudely carved their names in block letters in the wood, as if to prove to the future that they once existed: JIMMY, RANDY, DAVID, BOBBY, HARRY, VERNON, JOHN, SIMON . . . the post was covered with them.

What happened to them? Where did they go? Who did they become?

As if I'd asked that aloud, she said, "At least three of them are among my Romeos."

Mother meant those old boys who ate lunch together—not the opposites to her Juliet.

She sighed. "I'm just not getting any signals."

A bat swooped over our head.

"How's *that* for a signal!" I blurted. I took her by the arm. "Time for your bunions to declare defeat, and for us to get out of here."

We did.

Back in the kitchen, I thought we were leaving when Mother entered the spacious pantry and headed for a closed door.

"If *that* leads to the basement," I said firmly, "you're on your own."

Mother waved that off. "Dear, this isn't a scary movie. This is real life."

"*Scary* real life. . . . Go down there at your own peril."

Sushi sneezed as if in agreement.

"She may be buried below," Mother said, and opened the door, which creaked like a sound effect from an old radio show, stuck her head into the dark stairwell, then pulled it back.

"Very well," she announced. "You may have a point."

Whether she checked with her bunions before making that decision, I couldn't tell you.

"Thank you," I said.

We went back out through the window, and I replaced the boards as best I could. Sushi stayed with me, but Mother went off and I could hear her crunchy footsteps in the snow, breaking twigs and leaves.

I followed and found her in back, standing next to an old well.

"I'm getting something here, dear," she said, pointing down to her left foot.

Right. Couldn't just be that her bunions were hurting from all the tromping around we'd been doing.

The well, made of mortared stone, was about four feet high and about as wide across, with a heavy wood circular top.

"Help me with the lid, dear."

"Thirsty?"

"For a solution to the mystery, yes."

It took both of us to push the heavy cover off, where it hit the snowy ground with a thud.

We leaned over the edge and looked into darkness. Mother found a loose stone at the base, and tossed it down.

We heard neither splash nor thunk.

"That," I said, "is deep."

Mother said, "Deep enough to put a body down and not have it found."

I said, "Next you'll be saying Nurse Tanner is down there."

"She is," said a male voice behind us.

We turned to see Christopher Purdue, First National Bank Chairman himself, dressed in a navy pin-striped suit, sans topcoat, as if he had just stepped out of a board meeting.

I don't know if Mother was surprised by the banker's sudden presence, but I certainly was. Surprised and frightened, because he was holding in a casual hand a snub-nosed revolver, trained right at us.

He gestured with the weapon. "Cell phones down the well, please."

We complied.

Sushi was growling—whether she understood Purdue had a weapon or sensed our anxiety, I couldn't be sure; but I picked her up, holding her protectively, fearing as much for her safety as ours.

Mother said, "You lied to me, Christopher. You said you weren't an orphan."

Since Mother would hardly be indignant about a killer lying to her, I knew just what she was doing: speaking as she inched away from me so that the banker wouldn't have two close targets. If he shot at one of us, the other might have a chance to jump him. And I was the one without bunions.

Purdue's smile was strangely apologetic. "I didn't lie to you, Vivian—I *wasn't* an orphan. But I did live here for a few years after my mother got sick and couldn't take care of me . . . when I had no other relatives to go to."

He shifted his stance, but the gun still pointed our way.

He gave us an awful smile. "Miss Tanner loved to pick on the weaker boys, and I was somewhat sickly myself. She knew just where to hit us so the bruises wouldn't show. And if they did? If a bone got broken? Well, she'd say the clumsy boy just fell down the stairs." His laugh was harsh. "But every day I got stronger, and bigger, and one night, in the final days of this terrible place, when I was supposed to be in bed, I got her to chase me outside to the well, where I'd hidden a baseball bat. I was never happier in my life than when I clobbered that witch and pushed her down the well."

The coldness of his voice, the placidness of his expressionless face, made me shiver beyond anything the weather could do to me.

Mother said with sympathy, "Your actions were quite understandable, dear . . . however premeditated. You were a child, an abused child. People would have understood."

"Would they understand *today*, Vivian? There's no statute of limitations on murder, you know."

"But what would have pointed to you? Why

kill Simon to cover up a crime with which you would almost certainly never be connected? So *what* if the evil nurse's remains were found after all these years? There would be no forensics evidence left . . . surely nothing that could point to you."

Something sad, something haunted, flowed across his face. Something that he had lived with for a very long time.

"Oh, but you see, Vivian, there *was* something. As I started to push her into the well, unconscious, she came around, and grabbed the front of my shirt and ripped off the pocket . . . *a pocket that had my name on it.* It went down with her, tight in her grip. The name. *My* name."

The mistreated boy had signed his crime.

He shook his head. "No, I couldn't have Simon bringing in bulldozers that would dig up that well and make a discovery that would ruin my good name, my reputation, destroy a career I worked so hard to achieve. . . . So I kept an eye on the domestic violence center account, year after year, watching it grow slowly, certain that Simon would never get enough money to carry out his altruistic plan."

"And then, the night of the Stroll, at Hunter's," Mother said, "you overheard David Harper say his mother planned to donate that coin. Just toss it in Santa's bag. That would put the donation account over the top. And it pushed *you* over the top, too, didn't it, Chris? If Mildred Harper hadn't done that, Simon Wright would still be alive."

He could only nod. "Yes. And I wouldn't have been put into this . . . awkward position . . . now."

Mother, who had managed to put six or seven feet between us, made her move . . . and it was a bold one . . .

"Well," she said, impatiently, moving toward him, startling him, "*are* you going to kill us, or just stand around feeling sorry for yourself? If not, we're leaving. It's cold standing here. Come along, Brandy."

Mother marched right past the banker, making herself a target, allowing me time to take a run at him.

But Purdue didn't, and I didn't have to. He lowered the gun. And his head.

With Sushi in my arms I ran after Mother, kicking up snow. When I caught up with her, I looked back once to see Purdue sitting slumped on the edge of the well, then a second later took one last glance, and he was gone.

The following Tuesday afternoon, Mother and I were at our Trash 'n' Treasures shop, enjoying a brisk business selling various Christmas items, when Tony stopped in.

He was returning our cell phones, which had been retrieved from the bottom of the well, along with Purdue's body and the bones of Maude Tanner, with which the banker had become entwined on impact.

I got queasy at the notion of using the cell again, so I set it aside to recycle it. Mother, however, had no qualms about reclaiming hers.

"It would take me years to enter all my contacts again," she said later.

Right now Mother and I were behind the counter, Tony across.

"What's going to happen with the silver dollar?" I asked Serenity's chief. "Will it go back to Mrs. Harper?"

Tony said, "Technically it's the property of Simon Wright's estate. Dumpster Dan's out of luck because, thrown away or not, the coin was stolen property."

Mother said, "And Simon Wright's dream of a domestic violence center is out of luck, too, because the coin's worth never made it into the designated account."

I frowned. "Does that mean Della and Rod Conklin will get the coin?"

Mother said confidently, "A good lawyer could prevent that from happening by proving Mildred's intent."

"Moot point," Tony told us. "The Conklins stopped by the station this morning to say they're going to honor Della's father's intent, and fulfill Simon's dream."

Mother slapped the counter. "Well, you just *have* to love a happy ending!"

Tony straightened. "We're lucky this *did* have a 'happy ending,' Vivian. You and Brandy could have wound up at the bottom of that well yourselves."

Mother hopped off her stool. "I would simply love to discuss this with you further, Chief Cassato, and I do appreciate your implied thanks for clearing up another homicide for you. But for now, there's still one more box of Christmas decorations that need putting out before we close."

And she disappeared faster than Old St. Nick going up a chimney. Even one without an evil dead nurse stuffed up it.

I gave Tony half a smile. "Why do you bother?"

"I should make a New Year's resolution not to," he said wearily. Then a smile blossomed and he asked, "Dinner later? My place?"

"Love to." Picking up some greenery from the counter, I held it over my head.

Tony leaned forward, and I leaned in, and we kissed under the mistletoe.

Mother was right—don't you just have to love a happy ending?

A Trash 'n' Treasures Tip

Vintage ornaments add a special touch to any Yuletide tree, but make sure when using old lights that their cords and/or wires are not frayed. One year we used a set of 1950s Noma twinkle lights that did more than just twinkle—they set our live tree aflame. Oh Tannenbaum!

Don’t miss the next delightful

Trash ’n’ Treasures Mystery

ANTIQUES RAVIN’

Coming soon from Kensington Publishing Corp.

Keep reading to enjoy a sample excerpt . . .

Chapter One

Poe, Tallyho!

The dog days of August had arrived in Serenity, our sleepy little Iowa town nestled on the banks of the Mississippi River. Even at this early morning hour inside our two-story stucco house, with the air conditioner going full blast, I could tell it was going to be another hot and humid day.

At the moment, Mother and I were having breakfast in the dining room, at the Duncan Phyfe table, with Sushi on the floor next to me, waiting for any bites that I might drop by accident or on purpose. Sushi's idea of "dog days" is a 365-days-a-year proposition, in which heat and humidity are not a factor.

Mother is Vivian Borne, midseventies, Danish stock, her attractiveness hampered only slightly by large, out-of-fashion glasses that magnify her eyes, widowed, bipolar; a legendary local thespian, she is even more legendary in our environs as an amateur sleuth.

I am Brandy Borne, thirty-three, a blonde by choice, a Prozac-popping prodigal daughter who, postdivorce (my bad), crawled home from Chicago to live with Mother, seeking solitude and relaxation but finding herself (which is to say myself) the frequent if reluctant accomplice in Vivian Borne's mystery-solving escapades.

Sushi, whom you've already encountered, is my adorable diabetic shih tzu, whose diabetes-ravaged eyesight was restored by a cataract operation. Perhaps the smartest of our little trio, she is still taking daily insulin injections in trade for sugar-free treats.

For newbies just joining in—heaven help you. Life in Serenity isn't always serene, nor is it uneventful, meaning catching you up on the details is impractical. (Fortunately, all previous entries in these ongoing murder-mystery memoirs are in print.) Suffice it to say, best fasten your seat belt low and tight and just come along for the ride. That's what I do.

Longtime readers will recall that at the close of *Antiques Wanted,* Mother had been the only candidate left standing in the election for county sheriff, a race she'd won in a walk because it was too late for any last-minute competition. She'd won despite a campaign launched by Serenity's millennials to write in John Oliver, the comedian/commentator of *Last Week Tonight.*

This had irritated Mother no end. "He's *British*," she'd said again and again.

By the way, not revealing whom I voted for is my constitutional right. I believe it's called pleading the Fifth.

Mother's breakfast today was a typically Spartan one—grapefruit juice and coffee. Mine wasn't—pancakes with whipped cream and strawberries, bacon, orange juice, and coffee—but if ever a morning called for a sugar rush, protein, vitamin C, and caffeine, this was it.

Between bites, I asked, "How's the new communications system working?"

To my astonishment—and probably that of most townsfolk—Mother had kept her campaign promise to combine the separate dispatching systems of the police, sheriff, and fire departments into a single state-of-the art center that would handle all three, making the routing of 911 calls to the appropriate responder quicker and more efficient.

And she had done this—as also promised—at no cost to the taxpayers. How? By relentlessly going after grants for law enforcement and persuading—let's not call it blackmailing, shall we?—state representatives to assist her. These politicians knew that *she* knew they had skeletons in their closets they might not want to come rattling out. Okay, maybe call it blackmail . . . but implied blackmail.

Mother, after taking a sip of coffee, replied, "The new com sys is strictly ten-two. Thank you for asking, dear!"

"Ten to what? What are you talking about?"

"Ten-two is the police code for 'signal good.' You should familiarize yourself with all of them. I'll provide a cheat sheet!"

She removed a napkin from her collar, as if she was the one chowing down like a lumberjack. Serenity's new sheriff was dressed in a uniform of her own design, having tried on and rejected the scratchy, ill-fitting polyester one used by her predecessor, Pete Rudder. (To be clear, not the actual uniform he'd worn, but one supposedly in her size and for a female officer, though you'd never guess it.)

Anyway, Mother had contacted her favorite clothing company, Breckenridge, and—don't ask me how—had talked someone there into making several stylish jumpsuits of tan cotton/elastane with just the faintest hint of lavender, featuring plentiful pockets, epaulets, and subtle shoulder pads. The outfits also had horizontal nylon zippers at the elbows and knees that, when unzipped, would turn them into cooler (temp-wise) versions, which was how she was comfortably wearing one this steaming morning. (She still had the legs for it.)

I said, "I'm surprised you followed through with it."

Mother, about to take a sip of juice, frowned. "Followed through with what, dear?"

"The new communications center—especially one set up so that the public doesn't have access to it."

In the past, Mother had been able to walk into the PD and up to the Plexiglas, establish a rapport with the latest dispatcher, discover his or her weaknesses, then exploit those frailties to wheedle out confidential police information.

She gave me a smug little smile. "Well, dear, I'm on the *inside* now, and privy to everything."

I grunted. When her term of office ended, Mother might well come to regret the upgrade. If she ran for a second time, she would hardly be the only candidate for sheriff.

Her radio communicator, resting on the table, squawked, and she answered it.

"Ten-four, Deputy Chen," she said.

Deputy Charles Chen was her right-hand man. I feel sure that Charles's restaurateur parents were unaware of how close Chen was to Chan. Or maybe not—nobody called the handsome young deputy Charlie.

"Businesses in Antiqua got broken into overnight."

"A ten-twenty-two!"

"You want me to respond, Sheriff?"

"No, dear," Mother told him. "And do please call me Vivian. And now I'm off to Antiqua! It's time their mayor met the new county sheriff. Ten-nineteen—hold down the fort!"

"Okay."

"I believe you mean ten-four, dear."

The radio communicator clicked at her. She gave it a mildly offended look, then put it down and—eyes gleaming behind the large lenses—announced, "Time for us to roll, Brandy!"

What did I have to do with rolling, you may ask?

Well, due to her various vehicular infractions—

including but not limited to driving across a cornfield and knocking over a mailbox, both while off her medication—Sheriff Vivian Borne had no driver's license. . . . Well, actually she did. It just had REVOKED stamped on it.

Since the department couldn't spare a deputy just to haul her around, and the budget could not cover the cost of an outsider driver, she'd arm-twisted me into playing unpaid chauffeur.

And I wasn't happy about it.

We'd had to temporarily close our antiques shop, Trash 'n' Treasures—which, I guess, was okay, since August was always a slow month for sales, often with more money going out than coming in—but schlepping Mother around town and countryside was not my idea of a summer vacation.

Sushi had also been pressed into service, riding along with us, partly because the little furball was so cute and disarming. She was bound to put most people at ease when the sheriff came a-callin'.

But Soosh could also be very vindictive when left home alone for long periods of time—more than once Mother and I had returned to find a small cigar left in the foyer.

Mother had had a little jumpsuit made for her doggy deputy, as well, which had got only one day's wear before it was found shredded in the upstairs hallway, a mystery with no doubt as to who done it. I'd escaped any such indignity, my chauffeur's uniform being my own sundresses and sandals.

I had made it clear to Mother that my role was to be strictly unofficial. I wanted no uniform or badge or official designation. Anyway, what could sound more ridiculous than "Deputy Brandy"?

While I cleared the table, Mother put on her duty belt, of which she had two: a heavy one for serious situations, containing separate holders for her gun, nightstick, Taser, handcuffs, Mace, flashlight, and radio, plus pouches for bullets, Swiss Army knife, and latex gloves; and a lighter belt for investigations (like now), which included holders only for the radio and flashlight, and a large pouch for carrying antipsychotic pills, aspirin, antacids, allergy tablets, arthritis cream, eyedrops, laxatives, lip balm, and dog treats to make canine friends. (She wanted to take all her vitamins along, as well, but the pouch wouldn't close, and I purposely used a little cross-body purse so she couldn't load me down.) She had as yet never worn her heavier rig with sidearm, as it ruined the line of her uniform.

I was exhausted already, and we hadn't even left the house.

At a quarter to eight, Mother, Sushi, and I made the trek all the way outside and were immediately engulfed in oppressive heat. We trudged dutifully to her sheriff's car, parked in the driveway, doing our best not to wilt.

Mother had been given the choice of either a four-door Ford Taurus or a hatchback Ford Explorer. Both were white, with sky-blue sheriff's markings and the same policing equipment: in-car video system with monitor (mounted to the right of the rearview mirror), mobile data terminal (between the front seats and angled toward Mother), mobile radio system (beneath the dashboard), and standard steel mesh–Plexiglas barrier (between front and back seats). There was also a bunch of hardware in the wayback, like a battering ram (not as easy to use as seen on TV) and a canvas bag carrying a gas mask, protective boots, extra flashlights, and other items.

Since I wasn't an official law enforcement officer, I was prohibited from using any of this equipment, even if I knew how, which I didn't. Nor did I have any desire to.

Being the designated driver, I had lobbied for the Taurus, feeling more comfortable behind its wheel. But Mother had chosen the Explorer, which, I'd presumed, was because the larger vehicle looked more formidable and had four-wheel drive. The real reason for her preference for the SUV had soon become apparent—yesterday she had spotted a rusty metal 1950s lawn chair by the roadside and had commanded me to pull over and take custody of it, meaning put it in the hatchback.

Yes, folks, that's what I'm dealing with. And who the good people of Serenity County have protecting them.

Anyway, with me behind the wheel, Sushi on Mother's lap as the sheriff rode shotgun (not literally, though there was one in back), we headed out of Serenity—no siren wailing or lights flashing (that's 10-85, according to my cheat sheet)—bound for Antiqua.

Our destination was not a Caribbean island, but a little town located in the far western section of the county, just off Interstate 80, its sole industry the many antiques shops drawing tourists from all over the Midwest. Antiqua wasn't large enough to have its own police force, contracting instead with the county sheriff's department to provide certain services—patrolling the area, investigating crimes, handling traffic, and offering crime prevention classes.

To stay awake after the heavy breakfast, I asked, "How come we've never gone to Antiqua looking for merchandise? Sounds like it would be right up the Trash 'n' Treasures alley."

We'd made any number of trips to little towns around the region on buying expeditions, starting back in the days when we had a stall in an antiques mall, prior to our shopkeeper phase.

"Because even with our dealer's discount," Mother said, "the prices are too high."

When it came to hunting for bargains, Mother wasn't just a bottom-feeder; she was a subterranean gorger.

She went on, "Some of the shops in Antiqua used to be reasonable, and the occasional bargain could be sniffed out . . . but that was before Poe's Folly."

What do you think? Should I ask? Are you sure? Well . . . all right. But the responsibility is yours.

"What on earth," I asked, "is Poe's Folly?"

"Why, I'm surprised you've never heard of that, dear. It made news some years back. Quite a kerfuffle!"

I guess I'd been preoccupied with my own folly back in Chicago.

"One of the antique shops," she continued, "sold a small framed photo to a tourist for ninety dollars."

"That sounds a little high, but not the makings of anything newsworthy."

Mother lifted a finger. "Actually, it was a newsworthy *bargain*—a daguerreotype dating to eighteen fifty that turned out to be a rare portrait of Edgar Allan Poe himself."

"Worth *more* than ninety dollars . . ."

"Worth fifty-thousand simoleons."

"Ouch!"

Mother continued, "Needless to say, the incident—indeed dubbed 'Poe's Folly' by the media—was quite an embarrassment to the town, especially since the buyer took the picture to a taping of *Antiques Roadshow* in Des Moines, where the Antiqua shop's costly blunder was exposed to eight-point-five million viewers."

I smirked. "Must've been pretty embarrassing to the shop owner who sold it. Of course, it might encourage bargain hunters to drop by."

"One might think. But in fact it only called into question the shop's ability to price anything correctly . . . and I understand the owner hiked all his prices in self-defense. He took it hard."

"I thought any publicity was good publicity."

"Apparently not, dear. He killed himself." She went on cheerfully, death never anything that brought her down. "Anyhoo, after the folly became so widely known, prices skyrocketed all over town. No one wanted to make the same mistake twice!"

"Understandable," I said, "but probably not good for business."

She fluttered a hand. "Oh, initially, it had no effect, because bargain hunters came from hither and yon. But when nothing of significance was discovered beyond outrageous price tags, tourism dropped off significantly." She paused. "Then, a few years back, the town council concocted a plan to turn their folly into fortune."

"How'd they do that?" We were zipping along the interstate now, despite truck-heavy traffic.

"The first weekend in August, Antiqua holds Edgar Allan Poe Days, a gala three-day celebration, with festivities beginning on Friday."

"Well, that's tomorrow," I pointed out.

"Yes, and the pièce de résistance is a hunt for an authentic Poe collectible marked at a ridiculously low price."

"Like that daguerreotype photo?"

"Nothing quite so valuable, dear, but still worth a pretty penny. An ingenious gimmick to embrace its famous folly, don't you think?"

"Yes, but it must be tough coming up with Poe items like that."

"Not really. Everyone on the town council is an antiques dealer with beaucoup connections.

Last year's treasure was a short missive Eddie Poe had written to a friend about a change of address. Worth several thousand . . . priced at a mere twenty-five dollars."

"Not too shabby," I said. "How come we've never attended?"

Mother sniffed. "Because, dear, the first year the festival was held, I wrote to the city council and offered to perform 'The Raven' at the opening ceremony, in full costume and make-up!"

"As what? A raven?"

"Don't be ridiculous, dear! As Poe, of course. I look rather dashing in a mustache. And can you imagine? I never heard a peep back from them!"

"Ravens don't 'peep,' Mother. They squawk or something."

She was getting miffed about it all over again, enough so to get a curious upward look from Soosh. "Well, I *swore* to myself I would darken Antiqua's door nevermore!"

"But now you're sheriff, and you have to."

"And now they will see just who it was they underestimated!"

She didn't just hold a grudge; she caressed it, nurtured it. . . .

Fairly familiar with Poe's work, I said, "Maybe the issue was what a long poem 'The Raven' is. Maybe if you had offered up a shorter one, like 'Annabel Lee' or 'The City in the Sea' . . ."

But she was snoring.

Serenity County's new sheriff was starting her day off with a nap, as was the out-of-uniform deputy Sushi, curled in her lap.

The lady sleeps! Oh, may her sleep, / Which is enduring, so be deep!

I returned my attention to the road, where the gently rolling hills had been replaced with flat farmland, fields of tall green corn swaying seductively in the breeze, tassels ready for pollination.

Half an hour later an exit sign for Antiqua appeared, and I turned off the interstate onto a secondary road, where a gas station kept company with a cut-rate motel.

Soon a larger sign greeted me:

WELCOME TO ANTIQUA!

antiques capital
of the midwest
population 354

The asphalt road soon became the cobblestone of Antiques Drive, where well-kept houses on either side—some newer on the outskirts, some older more centrally placed—wore well-tended lawns in civic pride.

I passed a tree-shaded park with a large pond, several log cabin–style picnic shelters, and a perfunctory playground, both deserted at this early hour, then breezed on in to the small downtown. Mother and Sushi snored on.

I slowed the Explorer along the main drag to rubberneck at the quaint Victorian brick buildings decorated with colorful floral planters—

some hanging, others on windowsills—each business displaying its merchandise behind gleaming windows. Most were antiques stores, but here and there was a café or bakery or gift shop.

After three blocks the downtown turned residential again—houses not quite so nice now, but lawns still welcoming—and I backtracked along side streets, where more modern buildings maintained the town's service industries: drugstore, beauty shop, bar, and a branch bank. A clapboard church with small bell tower, that could have been built ten years ago or one hundred, was relegated to a side street, as well.

I was about to swing onto Antiques Drive again when a man in a pale yellow polo shirt and tan slacks ran into the street and flagged me down. He was smiling, but something frantic was in his expression.

I stopped and powered down the window, which was akin to opening a hot oven door.

"Ah . . . Sheriff?" the man asked, frowning. He was midsixties, silver-haired, and distinguished-looking (in a country-club way) and wore wire-framed glasses. Perhaps a sweet young thing like myself, in a sundress, was not what he was expecting.

"That would be her," I said, nodding to my uniformed if slumbering mother, a little drool oozing from her open mouth.

I poked her arm, and she woke up with a snort, echoed by Sushi. They looked at me with identical dazed expressions.

"What?" Mother mumbled. "Where?"

"Ten-twenty-three," I chirped, which meant we'd arrived at the scene, then turned back to the man. "Where do you want her?"

I admit it sounded a little like I was dropping off a potted plant.

"There," he said, pointing across the street to a one-story tan brick building, a sign above the entrance reading CITY HALL. Nothing antique or Victorian about the place, strictly modern-day institutional.

"We've been waiting for you," he went on, a tinge of irritation in his voice, which I attributed to the heat rather than to any perceived tardiness on our part, because we'd made good time, for not using the siren, anyway.

He turned and headed toward the building, while I pulled the car over to the curb.

Shutting off the engine, I said, "Hope city hall is air-conditioned."

Mother gave me a hard stare.

"What?" I asked.

"You *could* have woken me up!"

"I did wake you up."

"You could have woken me up *sooner.*" She was drying her mouth off with a hankie. "I had hoped to make a lasting first impression."

"Well, you succeeded."

We exited the vehicle, Mother carrying Sushi like a suspect she was hauling to the clink.

The interior of city hall was as dull and institutional as the exterior, with beige walls and tan-tiled floor. A large metal desk protected the offices of city officials behind it. On the desk was a multi-line phone, and a silver bell with RING FOR SERVICE, which suggested city hall had trouble keeping a receptionist.

The silver-haired man who'd flagged us down held out a hand to Mother. "I'm Myron Hatcher, the mayor, owner of Top Drawer Antiques."

Mother transferred Sushi to me, and shook the hand.

"Sheriff Vivian Borne," she said regally, not a speck of drool in sight. "And this is my ad hoc deputy, Brandy Borne. My daughter." She summoned a forced smile. "If the president can hire his family, so can I!"

I didn't care for the deputy designation, ad hoc or otherwise, but I had no need to embarrass her—she could handle that without my help.

When the mayor's hand went to me, I transferred Sushi back to Mother and shook with him myself.

All this transferring had annoyed Sushi, who growled, and squirmed out of Mother's arms.

Mr. Hatcher was saying, "Please come on back."

We skirted around the big desk and proceeded down the beige hallway, passing doors reading "Mayor," "Treasurer," and "Administrator." At one marked, "Conference," our host opened the door, and we proceeded in, Sushi trotting in last.

The bulk of the room was taken up by an oval-shaped table with seating for about a dozen, four of which were occupied by two men and two women.

"Sheriff," Mr. Hatcher said. "I'd like you to meet the members of the city council."

Mother nodded regally to them, a queen to her court. "I would like that myself."

Since I was now out of the conversation, I parked myself on a small couch in the corner, where Sushi soon joined me.

The mayor began the introductions.

The council consisted of Lottie Everhart, late forties, long dark hair, attractive, attired in a leopard-print dress, owner of Somewhere in Time; Rick Wheeler, thirties, handsome, blond, buff in a tight white T-shirt and black jeans, manager of Treasure Aisles Antiques Mall; Wally Thorp, midfifties, round-faced, overweight, thinning gray hair, sporting a short-sleeved plaid shirt and cargo shorts, proprietor of Junk 'n' Stuff; and Paula Baxter, early fifties, short dyed red hair, rather plain-faced, in part due to scant make-up, wearing a sleeveless navy cotton dress, owner of Relics Antiques.

With the preamble concluded, Mother took a chair next to Paula, while the mayor put a few empty seats between himself and the others.

"Now," Mother said, "who wants to fill me in?"

The council members deferred to the mayor.

"As far as we can tell," Myron said, "our five shops were entered through the back entrances sometime last night."

Mother nodded. "What about security systems?"

Rick said sourly, "They don't do any good when the sheriff's department is an hour away."

"A valid point," Mother conceded. "Though

just a loud alarm can be helpful. Have you been able to determine what was stolen?"

Paula turned up both palms. "*Nothing* seems to have been taken from mine."

"Or mine," added Lottie.

"Same here," Myron said.

Wally, the junk store owner, smirked, "It would take me a week of Sundays to take stock of my stock."

Mother looked at Rick. "What about you, young man?"

"I've contacted all my dealers in the mall," he said, with a shrug, "but most haven't had a chance to take an inventory yet." His eyebrows went up. "But I did a walk-through, and everything *looked* okay."

Myron spoke. "Strikes us as odd, Sheriff, that all our registers had cash in them, which went untouched. No small fortune, even combined . . . but still, why would a thief not help himself?"

"Or herself," Mother said, with a grave nod.

Paula piped up. "I expected to find my glass case with expensive rings and watches broken into and emptied out, but it wasn't."

"Nor," Lottie said, "was any of my rare Roseville pottery missing."

When Mother's eyes went to Wally, he merely shrugged; apparently the junk-man had nothing of real value in his store.

Mother rested her elbow on the table and her chin on a hand. "What do you think the burglar was after?"

Again, the group yielded to the mayor. "The

only thing we can figure is that someone went looking for this year's Poe item . . . knowing it would be a valuable prize."

"Makes sense. And what would that prize be?"

The question drew silence and shared wary looks within the group.

Then Myron spoke. "Sorry, Sheriff Borne . . . but we're really not at liberty to say. You see, the first of three encrypted clues as to what the Poe prize is won't be released to the public until tomorrow, at the opening ceremony."

"Myron, this is the *sheriff*," Paula chided. "I think she can be trusted with the information."

Wondering if my presence might be a problem, I offered to leave the room.

But the mayor shook his head. "Not necessary, Deputy."

Deputy. I didn't love the sound of that.

Adjusting his wire frames again, the major sighed, then said, "Very well. It's a book called *Tales*, published in eighteen forty-five by Wiley and Putnam, featuring perhaps the author's most famous story, 'The Gold-Bug.'"

Lottie sat forward. "That's where we got the idea for the encrypted clues," she said. "The first one says what the value of the prize is, the second one tells what it is, and the third gives the antiques shop where the book is hidden among various merchandise on display."

Mother was taking this in through narrowed eyes. "It does sound as though the burglar wanted to get a jump on the competition."

"Yes," Wally said. "Only he . . . or she . . . didn't know we'd changed the procedure this year."

"How so?"

"We aren't hiding the prize until the second day of the festival."

"That was by necessity," Lottie said. "Last year the letter was found right away, and that cast a cloud over the rest of the weekend."

Paula was nodding. "People left. And our shops didn't do at all well on a weekend that's bigger than Christmas for Antiqua."

"City hall especially suffered," the mayor added.

I heard myself say, "This doesn't look like an antiques shop to me."

The mayor glanced over at me. "No, but we usually do a big business on Poe weekend. We offer deciphered clues for ten dollars a pop, and a lot of people prefer paying the cash rather than figuring out the cryptograms—which we depend on to fund our *next* year's prize of a Poe rarity."

Rick rolled his eyes, his expression glum. "We merchants had to dig into our own pockets this year."

The room fell silent again.

"Perhaps," Mother suggested, "you should have some law enforcement presence during the festival."

The mayor looked startled. "That might alarm folks."

I had been feeling guilty about making Mother look like a buffoon by not waking her up, so I piped up.

"Sheriff Borne does a wonderful reading of

'The Raven,'" I said. "If you asked her to perform at the opening ceremony, it would make perfect sense for her to be around all weekend. She could be an honored guest."

When the council agreed my idea was a good one, Mother sent me a grateful look.

Since the members needed to open their shops soon, the meeting came to an end, Mother shaking hands and exchanging smiles all around.

When Mother informed them she wanted to examine the rear of those shops to see how the burglar had gained entrance, I told her Sushi and I would be at a little coffee shop down the street that I'd noticed.

Mother stopped me with a hand on my arm. She whispered, "There's something I am particularly concerned about."

"What's that?"

"I really don't think my Poe mustache will go very well with my uniform."

For a moment I thought she was joking, but then I remembered she had no sense of humor. Rather, she spread laughter around, a Typhoid Mary of comedy.

"Mother," I said seriously, "I believe you have the acting chops to *imply* a mustache."

Mother was nodding at that as I walked out with Lottie, who handed me a piece of paper.

"Here's what the encrypted first clue looks like," she said, then added, with a good-natured smile, "If you want a deciphered one, it'll cost you ten bucks."

I looked at the row of numbers and symbols . . . and coughed up the tenspot for a second slip of paper with the solution. Even an ad hoc deputy can put in for a few expenses.

Lottie said, "The numbers and symbols are random designations of letters, but the code is consistent throughout the next two clues. So with this, you should be able to figure out the others."

A savings for the county of twenty bucks. Now I was a fiscally responsible ad hoc deputy.

The outside of the Coffee Club looked more upscale than the inside, with its worn carpet, scarred prefab tables, and cracked faux-leather padded chairs. But none of that mattered, because the air-conditioning was nicely arctic.

I spotted a waitress behind the counter, early twenties, with short, spiky purple hair, alabaster skin, purple lipstick. Just another typical small-town girl.

Still in the doorway, I asked, "Is it okay if my dog comes in?"

She shrugged. "Since the boss isn't here, sure."

I took a table for two and placed the panting Sushi in my lap.

The waitress came over. Her name tag said MORELLA, and she reeked of Shalimar perfume. Hanging from her neck on a silver chain was a pendent of a black raven, wings spread.

"And how are you?" I asked pleasantly.

"Livin' the dream. What can I get you?"

"Iced coffee . . . and maybe a little water for Sushi?"

"Right." She headed back behind the counter.

A few other customers occupied tables—two giggling teenage girls hunched over a cell phone, and a young mother with a small boy eating cupcakes.

Morella returned and set a sweating glass in front of me and a little bowl of water before Soosh. Sushi's tongue flicked out and lapped up the liquid loudly.

"Thanks," I said. "Nice town."

"Don't look under the hood."

"Well, the people seem friendly enough."

One heavily filled-in eyebrow went up. "Do they?"

"So far."

"Stick around."

Bluntly, I asked, "What keeps you in this town?"

"As soon as I get enough money, nothing."

"Destination?"

She flashed something that was probably a smile. "Anywhere else."

Morella put my ticket on the table, then went to check on the other customers.

While I sipped my cold drink, I spread out the two slips of paper Lottie had given me—the cryptogram and its solution.

;48 [50?8 +1 ;48 6;89 6) ;8 ;4+?)5*=*

I took a pen from my little bag to make notes, recording which random numbers and symbols stood for which letter. Even without the ten-dollar translation, the code seemed pretty easy—a semicolon equaled a "t," a 4 equaled an "h," and 8 equaled an "e" (adding up to "the"). Also, spaces between the symbols indicated separate words, which wasn't the case in "The Gold-Bug," meaning when I got the next cryptogram, I could probably save Serenity County ten bucks.

On the other hand, ten thousand bucks seemed like a lot for the local merchants to shell out.

The value of the item is ten thousand.

I finished the iced coffee, left cash for the drink, plus a generous tip to speed Morella on her way anywhere else, and Sushi and I departed.

Going back to join Mother, I crossed the side street where our Explorer was parked across from city hall.

A slip of paper pinned beneath a wiper waved hello in the warm breeze. Walking through heat shimmering off the sidewalk, I went to the vehicle, plucked off the note.

This message needed no deciphering.

Believe nothing you hear and only half of what you see. Edgar Allan Poe.

A Trash 'n' Treasures Tip

When collecting rare books, first decide if you will hunt on your own or use a reputable book dealer. If you hunt on your own, you will pay less, but you will be on your own. Unless you are very well schooled in the hobby, you may mistake a later edition for a first. A dealer will hunt for you and protect you from such mistakes, but expect to pay higher prices. On the other hand, Mother once paid thirty dollars for a Rex Stout first edition worth fifteen hundred dollars (books were on sale 20 percent off, and Mother insisted on her discount).